THE END, MY FRIEND

Prelude to the Apocalypse

Kirby Wright

Published by Lemon Shark Press
San Diego, California
www.lemonsharkpress.com
ISBN: 0974106798
ISBN-13: 978-0974106793
Copyright © 2013 by Kirby Wright
All Rights Reserved

**LEMON SHARK
PRESS**

In memory of Katherine Hirneisen

Somewhere over the rainbow

Tim will find you

CONTENTS

Prologue

Epilogue

ACKNOWLEGEMENTS
Love and gratitude to Darcy for believing.

PROLOGUE

I WANT TO TELL YOU how we lost everything. Fear and greed triggered a meltdown of epic proportions, a catastrophe exceeding all the wars and acts of God combined. Everything we took for granted we destroyed. Every day became a fight for survival. Millions perished in the ruins. The only choice was to flee with my family for the Northern Territories. My story's not for the faint of heart. So, if you're easily upset, read no more. But if you want the truth from an ordinary guy at ground zero, it wouldn't hurt to go on. Maybe you can help bring back the world we once shared, or at least the part worth saving.

*   *   *

Killer asteroids, tsunamis, or perfect storms didn't doom us. Forget zombies, flesh-eating bacteria, or nuclear fires. It was something more insidious, something that gnawed away at the fabric of civilization and lured our primal selves to the surface. We'd just re-elected the President in a landslide when our rights and privileges vanished in an economic downturn sweeping coast to coast. Americans realized they were living in a prison called the United States, a country controlled by the rich through industry, finance, real estate, food, and water. Advances in robotic labor decimated the job market. New laws favoring the wealthy punished the middle class.

1

Savings dwindled. Fuel prices skyrocketed and inflation doubled the price of food in less than a year. PRISM extended its reach beyond National Security issues to violate a score of constitutional clauses. Peaceful marches became demonstrations. Demonstrations turned into riots. Riots escalated into prolonged battles pitting patriots against the police and squads of humanoid robots. Inner cities reeked of tear gas. The economy reeled with steep losses in technology, commodities, and industry. The Fed incinerated the Occupy camps. Patriots fought back by dismantling urban infrastructure and creating food banks for the New Poor. Panic spread to Europe. Foreign governments and monetary systems teetered on the brink of collapse as economic cyclones wreaked havoc. A Munich rally against government rationing became a murderous rampage when Germans challenged the Polizei. Tuscan peasants rose up against oppressive landowners. Parisians torched the Eiffel Tower and looted hotels. Palestinians ravaged settlements in East Jerusalem. Tracks were ripped up along Spain's Almerian coast. Bombs leveled Buckingham Palace. Resistors stormed St. Petersburg. The Jewish Quarter in Prague became a staging area for rebel forces in Eastern Europe. The President called an emergency G-20 Summit in New York, but the world leaders failed to agree on a plan to stabilize the continents. Patriots stirred up a mob that triggered a blood bath on Wall Street. The President outlawed private ownership of guns. Weapon depositories were established in every city and town—getting caught with a gun meant a mandatory ten years in prison. The New Poor marched from the Lincoln Memorial to the White House with FUCK THE FED banners. The financial meltdown destroyed stocks and bonds. Millions of homes foreclosed. The World Bank quit lending.

The Middle East became the world's black market. Gas hit $50-a-gallon. The markets of Germany, Greece, and Portugal collapsed. Borders blurred with massive refugee influxes. Chemtrails circled the globe. Priests and ministers preached The Book of Revelation, especially passages about angels spilling bowls of rage. The Massacre at Red Square inspired a revolt so fierce Russia begged the U.S. for help. The President offered shipments of corn and wheat.

Russia was the first major to fall. Anarchy swept through Europe and reached Asia. North Korea nuked South Korea and the U.S. retaliated by leveling Pyongyang. Patriots in *V for Vendetta* masks hurled Molotov cocktails at the White House before the Secret Service gunned them down. The Fed arrested anyone labeled "subversive." The NSA continued mining stockpiles of wireless data to satisfy PRISM. Americans were spied upon in every way imaginable, and arrested for crimes they didn't commit. Military bases became federal prisons. When all available cells were full, Tent Prisons were built on tracts of fallow land and in the farthest reaches of the deserts.

Politicians in all the states, cities, and counties became targets. America fell two months after the President was assassinated.

BOOK 1

CALIFORNIA

PORTICO

MY NAME IS TONY Pernicano. I was born in the Bronx. I've been on my own since dropping out of high school. I worked my way across the country doing odd jobs, everything from shoveling manure in Kentucky to picking corn in Nebraska to working as an orderly in Santa Fe. I scrimped and saved enough to move to California. I bought a bar in Oceanside the day I turned thirty.

I'm a far cry from the Italian hunks you see in movies. My snozolla is huge and I have beady eyes. I could lose some weight. Evo, my better half, is a Norwegian beauty. How we ended up together is the mystery of my life. She saw me surfing in Carlsbad and asked for a lesson. One thing led to another and now, two years later, Evo's one month along. Her due date's the Winter Solstice. Sudzy, our cat, is great practice for the baby. "The princess" cries for meals and purrs whenever I rock her in my arms.

We live in Vista, a city due east of the Pacific. Our realtor had me when she said it was "a Mediterranean climate." We're close enough to the coast to smell the salty brine of the ocean. Portico is our subdivision. All the homes have peach stucco walls with red-tiled roofs. The tiles remind me of scales. I tell Evo we're one in a school of happy red fish. We shop at Albertsons, cheer for the Chargers, and bid on eBay. The only downside is hearing the *boomah-boom-boom* reverbs from F-18s practice-bombing the Whiskey and Zulu regions of Camp Pendleton. The windows rattle like tambourines and Sudzy bolts. Hawks in our Torrey pine screech at the planets and stars.

*   *   *

All hell broke loose the day the VP took the Presidential oath. Not that hell wasn't already unleashed after the assassination, with skirmishes between the New Poor and the Fed. The FDIC quit honoring guarantees, and people who thought they had money were suddenly broke. Lines wrapped around banks. Hospitals gave doctors and nurses pink slips. Restaurants quit serving. City and county offices locked their doors. Fear triggered violence in the Land of the Free. The police quit answering emergency calls. Firemen watched cities and towns burn. The internet went kaput. Schools closed.

Kids tore through Portico on dirt bikes and skateboards into the early morning hours. Neighbors became reclusive. Everyone ate from cans—favorites were pork & beans, beef stew, ravioli, sardines, and tuna. Rice, beans, and noodles were a hoarder's delight. Batteries, toilet paper, and charcoal disappeared from store shelves. Growing fruits and vegetables caught on, but Portico's residents approached it with such desperation that most seedlings either withered or got drowned by over-watering. A few neighbors fished. Others trapped squirrels, rabbits, and raccoons. Mr. Hadulco cooked a tasty stew he'd made with garlic, onions, carrots, and snake meat. A boy snared a possum and his grandmother baked a possum potpie. We heard strange animal sounds at night—mercy howls and cries for life before the butchering.

We had plenty of canned goods so there was no need to fish or trap. Evo's garden was loaded with cherry tomatoes, butter lettuce, and kale. The trees on our hill were heavy with oranges. We had jugs of bottled water and cases of canned cat food. Heebie and Jeebie, our red ear slider turtles, ate earthworms and snails.

We were better off than most. Fathers went door-to-door begging. Some carried babies for sympathy and one tried tricking me with a doll. I gave what we could. I caught Fritz, our neighbor to the west, yanking oranges off a tree on my hill.

"Whatcha doing, Fritz?" I called up.

"Just borrowing," he stammered.

What a dickweed. I let him keep what he'd picked but warned Fritz that, during the next fruit thief episode, he'd taste a knuckle sandwich. He smiled. I guess he figured his 300-pound housebound son would protect him. After Fritz left, I tied aluminum cans to the branches. Old Man Darwin, three doors down, gave me that idea. He'd fired his revolver when cans clanged on his peach tree and the tree never clanged again.

Our Portico women gave up makeup, coloring their hair, getting tans, and shaving. They aged a decade in a single season. Cougar Joan's hair turned to ash. Mary the Crone became a dead ringer for the Grim Reaper. Buxom Betty's legs sprouted a five o'clock shadow. Evo was a rare exception—she never wore makeup anyway and rarely messed with her short, ginger brown hair. But she continued shaving her legs.

The HOA hosted a dinner party trying to restore some semblance of normalcy. The director strung up a cow off a coral tree on Longhorn Drive and a former chef carved it up. Fritz trucked in mesquite and families congregated at the Rancho Buena Vista stadium for a barbecue with all the fixings. There was Iron Fist beer, coconut-flavored tequila, and free lemon soap. Men carried rifles. A girl announced her engagement. Keith the Postman showed up with his band and everyone danced to the Oldies. That event seemed to lift Portico out of the doldrums, and it felt as though we'd make it through tough times if we all stuck together.

The post barbecue glow dimmed soon after the lights went out. No-gas and no-water followed. It seemed only temporary, as if lights would re-ignite, gas would swirl in to let us cook, and water would cascade happily through the pipes. Landlines and cell phones became inoperative. Wi-Fi vanished. Only GPS worked.

Evo and I made the best of Portico deconstructing. It was romantic eating pork & beans by candlelight and hugging her for warmth. There were no distractions. We drank chardonnay and kissed. I rubbed her belly. She nibbled my ear. The crickets feasted on the darkness—their *crick-cricketing* brought me back to camping days with Dadio, my father, and my little bro, Jimmy. Evo loved the crickets. We could hear neighbors telling stories and laughing, as if we were all scouts camping under the stars over a long weekend. But our camp-out dragged on for weeks and no-utilities darkened everyone's spirits. No-gas meant no heat. Not that we really needed it in San Diego County. But the rains lingered through Palm Sunday and everyone was cold and miserable. Some dismantled fences to feed fireplaces. We slipped under comforters. Evo suggested flying to Oslo to stay with her parents. Knute, Evo's father, told us the Russians were on Norway's doorstep and not to come. A week later, all domestic and international flights were grounded. The Transit Center in Oceanside became a holding tank for convicts headed by train for Camp Fema in Torrance, a former military base.

Voices started tumbling down the hill—monologues filled with bravado and passionate plans for survival. I figured neighbors were rambling to kill the fear. I'd hear "wait it out," "no more water," and "gotta get guns." Two brothers with rifles became fixtures on a balcony. Their mother was always yelling at them to make their beds.

The first wave of the New Poor descended on Vista Business Park. Most were locals who'd been evicted before the banks went bust. Clans from Arizona and Nevada joined them. They'd burn rubbish in oil drums and cook over the flames. A mechanic told me an army of ex-cons, derelicts, and vets was forming in Phoenix, and that they'd swollen their ranks by overwhelming Camp Fema on the outskirts of the city and a Tent Prison near Yuma.

Candlelight at Portico became the norm. The first generators appeared and all available gas ended up in their bellies. Neighbors lit up their homes like birthday cakes. The generators *put-ah-putted* all night and it seemed as if we were living in a construction zone. Evo suffered from insomnia. Sudzy hid. Fritz asked if I wanted to hook up to his generator for "a nominal fee."

"How much is 'nominal?'" I asked.

"All the oranges, plus ten ounces of gold."

"I don't have gold."

"Any canned ham?"

"Forget it, Fritz."

"Suit yourself, Tony. But I'm sure Evo would enjoy having some light."

Evo told me candlelight suited her just fine. Good thing too— Portico returned to the Dark Ages when the gas ran out. Mark the Stooge said he was considering putting his mother in a kennel from dusk to dawn because she went "nutso" in the dark.

Neighbors used the water in pools, Jacuzzis, and hot tubs for bathing. When their bottled water ran out they boiled pool water and drank it, even though algae had invaded. People scoured yards for forgotten buckets hoping to find rainwater. Some drank from aquariums and fried finned pets on propane stoves. Catchment caught on. Elaborate gutters and terraced hillsides funneled rain into barrels and buckets. Outhouses sprang up.

We didn't need an outhouse. We had plenty of water from a 100-gallon catchment barrel I'd rigged in January. My first chore every morning was filling plastic one-gallon jugs, lugging them up to our second floor bathroom, and filling the toilet tank. Sometimes the water had mosquito worms but that didn't matter. After toilet duty, I watered the garden and the fruit trees. I let the yard go. The lawn turned yellow in a week. Ferns, roses, and hibiscus wilted, not to mention the poinsettias. The ice plant held on.

Portico's cell phone tower became a climbing wall for skinheads. One tied a Nazi flag to the tower. A vet picked him off with a rifle. The skinhead brethren strung up the vet by his ankles on an ash tree and hacked him with an ax. There was nothing I could do without getting axed myself. Fritz lowered the shades on his windows.

Kids went door-to-door at night. The leaders had guns. The new craze was blasting out the windows of those who'd been stingy on Halloween. Even though I was known for being generous, I still boarded up our windows. A tween got shot breaking and entering, but most ended up with the loot. You know that sweet spot in your home where you stash the valuables? They found it. And, if they didn't, they threatened to burn you down if you refused to cough up the family jewels.

"Never open the door," I told Evo.

"Not even for the Jehovahs?" she asked.

Riots became the norm. A few hundred rioters swelled to thousands when gangs and militias joined them. San Diego's Finest unleashed a steady diet on the mobs—water cannons, tear gas, mace, pepper spray, plastic bullets, and Tasers. The coast smelled like poison.

Martial law was imposed. Camp Fema San Diego was established in Otay Mesa, the former home of the George Bailey Prison. Fences around the prison reached forty feet and were crowned with razor wire. National Guardsmen had shoot-to kill-orders. Combat teams that were deployed overseas returned to curb civil unrest. A gang leader detonated grenades inside a National Guard barracks and killed a General. The bombing runs ended at Camp Pendleton. The U.S. Army was ordered south to stop illegals flooding over from Tijuana. The VP sent in drones to incinerate Revolution Boulevard but, heat-seeking missiles blew the drones out of the Tijuana sky. A surprise battalion of Mexican soldiers stormed the border and freed the prisoners at Camp Fema. The prisoners joined the Mexicans. One prisoner was a special ops expert, and he wired a mega-bomb that took out a dozen U.S. tanks and two fighter jets. Mexico advanced north with heavy artillery and foot soldiers. The Marines backed off. It was Earth Day, and the Mexican flag flew over Imperial Beach.

The rich in the coastal cities of La Jolla and Del Mar pooled their money and hired private security run by an ex-Seal. Checkpoints were set up along Pacific Coast Highway. You had to prove you lived there to get through. The coastal grid failed. Back-up generators died when the gas ran out, and solar generators couldn't handle the demand. The ex-Seal and his men battled armed gangs coming up from the beaches and down from the hills. Mansions got plundered.

Evo and I listened to radio reports of teenage warlords carving out territories from Cardiff to Chula Vista. Guns were at a premium. Radio died and we could only imagine what was going on.

*　　　*　　　*

Fritz climbed onto the roof of his motor coach and bragged he'd build a superior society called "Green City" in the Mohave. Mary the

Crone and Old Man Darwin chanted, "Green City, Green City." Mark the Stooge joined Fritz on the roof and they pumped their fists. Cougar Joan danced with Keith the Postman. Somehow I couldn't envision a village, or even a handful of tents, in a desert wasteland. Fritz organized a caravan of cars, trucks, and SUVs and they all met in the Rancho Buena Vista parking lot. He led the way in his motor coach flying Green City flags. There were honks, cheers, and music as they followed Fritz down Longhorn Drive toward the I-15. My neighbors were off to build a commune. It was late April and the desert plains were masterpieces of flowers, sage, and lavender. I was tempted to follow, until Evo reminded me the Mohave's as dry as a bone.

"They don't call it 'the Badlands' for nothing," she said.

The Badlands. That drove home the point. A week later, a vicious Santa Ana knocked the fruit off our trees. The leaves on the coral tree got fried and the ice plant wilted.

"Glad we didn't go?" Evo asked.

The Green City families didn't last long. Old Man Darwin returned and said they'd run out of water. Some drank urine and sucked cacti. Mark the Stooge guzzled anti-freeze before running naked toward a mirage he swore was a lake. Fritz sold his grandson for a case of Red Bull and a side of bacon.

ROVY

WE'VE GOT TWENTY gallons left in our rain barrel. I'll drive to Mobraaten Pond if we get any lower. Pond water's safe, but you've got to boil it first and strain out impurities with a coffee filter.

*   *   *

Gangs hit two homes last night in Portico. I shouldn't be concerned because only a quarter of the homes are still occupied. I sleep sporadically and keep a metal bat on my nightstand. Evo has an iron skillet under her side of the bed. Voices continue rolling down the hill—lots of cussing and survivalist chatter. Beer cans tossed from above are stuck in the branches of our trees.

*   *   *

Pyramids of trash rise from the gutters. Rats scavenge by daylight. I stroll out when I spot Keith the Postman sledgehammering a safe on the curb. Andy Gap, a skinny kid, says it's his mother's safe but that she spaced out the combination.

"Batter up," Keith announces. He hits the safe so hard the dial flies off. The tiny door pops and a stream of gold spills over the sidewalk.

"Sick!" squeals Andy, digging through the loot.

14

"My reward?" Keith asks.

Andy flips him a Gold Eagle.

"What about me?" I go.

Andy frowns. "You didn't help, dude."

*   *   *

My cousin Derek owns a cabin in Crestline. Before the phone died, he said we could stay with him "until the dust settled."

"Crestline?" I ask Evo.

She nods. "We're sitting ducks here at Portico."

*   *   *

I pull on my black tank and pewter shorts. I head downstairs, mosey past Evo in the kitchen, and slip into my rubber slippers out in the garage. I keep the garage door closed because you're an easy target if thieves know you're busy packing and putting everything valuable in one place.

Five-gallon water jugs are lined up behind Rovy, our white Land Rover Discovery. I swing open the cargo door and lift one in. Six more follow. Next comes a pair of sleeping bags, a toolbox, road flares, a floor jack, a rod and reel, a tackle box, jumper cables, wetsuits, a solar-powered battery charger, antifreeze, and Royal Purple motor oil. I toss in my hydraulic nail gun. I pack power steering fluid, gear oil, tranny fluid, and two suitcases. I stick a leather pouch filled with silver bullion and coins in the glove box. I pile in bags of rice and potatoes, pasta, and 12-packs of Snickers. In goes a box of cowboy matches, cans of propane, and a Coleman stove. I drop the GPS into the center console.

Evo lugs out cat stuff: a bucket of sand, a shoebox for poop, a pooper scooper, fur ball remedy in a tube, canned food, a bottle of chemo pills, and latex gloves. Sudzy's pills help her battle lymphatic cancer. Radiation would leach through the casings and enter my bloodstream without the gloves.

Evo's got cardboard boxes stuffed with linen postcards, antique dolls, anointing spoons from English coronations, Dutch cake servers, hand-blown Murano bowls, crystal decanters, and antique copper switch plates. She plans on taking her uranium glass collection, but no way is there room for that. She's also boxed an assortment of figurines, vases, plates, salt and peppershakers, and Howdy Doody toothpick holders. She insists on taking her spoons with painted bowls, including the one with a portrait of Marie Antoinette.

"We could use the spoons to barter," she decides.

I wince. "Who'd want those?"

"They're pure silver."

"Silver plated," I go, "practically worthless."

"Most are sterling. Some are gold washed."

"You win," I concede.

Evo ducks back in the house and returns with her big blue

exercise ball. She likes rolling around on it in our living room, in front of a wooden Buddha.

"No ball," I grouch.

"It deflates, Tony."

"You'll need the Incredible Hulk to blow it back up."

"Gas stations have air."

"It's either Sudzy or the ball."

"I have to choose between my ball and our Russian Blue?"

"I hope you choose the Russian."

"Should I leave behind my wedding ring?"

"Very funny," I go. I gave Evo a five-carat orange tourmaline ring with accent diamonds, in an art deco design.

Evo crosses her arms. "What about my Buddha?"

"What about him?"

"He was our anniversary gift from Knute."

"I could strap fatso to the roof rack."

Evo smiles. "Good karma," she promises and heads back inside.

I pack a FatMax fubar that looks like a hooligan's tool, a Kukri machete, a Eureka 3-person dome tent, and an aluminum mess kit. I find my old brass canteen and stick it under the passenger seat. Next come the guns. I wrap a wetsuit around the DPMS Panther and slip it between the Royal Purple and the stove. The Panther is my mid-long range rifle, with a gloss black barrel over three feet long and a sniper scope. This semi-auto's ten pounds and fires a .308 round. Long-range capabilities are vital. It's best to kill from a distance, before enemies get close enough to hurt you. Survival means firepower and accuracy. My second weapon is Super Shorty, a snub-nosed shotgun, my choice for up close and personal. It holds ten shells and the short barrel intensifies the kick. I slip it in the driver's door compartment. Third, but not least, is the Beretta Sub Compact. I pluck it off the pegboard above the chainsaw. It belonged to Dadio. The Beretta's not registered, but registering's the last thing you do these days. The gun's easy to conceal and discharges a deadly 9 mm round. It holds fourteen, with one in the chamber. This one's primarily for close combat, but it also has mid-range accuracy. I slip a holster over my right shoulder and stick the Beretta in. All I need to do is reach across with my left to draw. I pack ammo for all three guns. Finally, I toss in my East German bayonet with the serrated edge and black Bakelite handle—the steel still has a slick layer of protective Cosmoline from the Cold War. The blade fits snugly inside a black plastic sheath.

I know insecure men carry weapons. I also know if you get mad at someone and have a gun or a blade you get tempted. But suppose a punk with a gun wants you dead? Imagine if that hippie in *Easy Rider* had a gun when those rednecks pulled alongside? A guy without a gun is dead meat.

Next in are Heebie and Jeebie, my aquatic turtles. Heebie's the boy and Jeebie's the girl. They're in my Igloo cooler. I adopted them years ago from Dave, my teacher pal, after his third graders quit caring for them. I wedge the cooler between the nail gun and the wet-suited Panther.

Evo appears. She buckles on her fanny pack, hops in the passenger seat, and places the carrier on the rubber mat. Evo's got on a green tankini, black shorts, and leopard sneakers. She drags Sudzy out of the carrier. "Beam us up, Scotty," she says, plopping the princess on her lap.

I press the remote clipped to the visor and the garage door creaks up. I turn the key—the engine purrs. I'm relieved that our child isn't due until Winter Solstice. A baby can slow you down on the road and make you vulnerable because you get overly preoccupied—feeding, fretting, and changing diapers. I gaze through the wing mirror—our street's deserted. "To Crestline," I mumble, clicking the shifter into reverse. I wonder what the future holds in the new world.

OLD BRAT ON THE BLOCK

EVO HATES GUNS. I told her everyone has one. Why, even Mary the Crone sleeps with her dead hubby's Luger. Mr. Garza blew off a punk's thumb last Friday with his .38 semi-auto. Funny how movie heroes always have time to load and cock hammers before big shootouts. I'm taking no chances—I've got Super Shorty's chamber stuffed with buckshot.

I ease out to Marbella Drive. Rovy's tires grip the asphalt. Doves peck at grains of rice while a hawk watches from a chimney perch. I tool through the burbs, toward a shirtless teen squatting on the curb. It's Ryan, the brat I told to beat it when he skateboarded our driveway. A green F-150 sits in the fire lane. Ryan spots us. He leaps in the truck, fires it up, and cranks the wheel hard until he's blocking the road.

I power down my window.

"Easy does it, Tone," says Evo.

Ryan ransacked the Wongs yesterday. Dr. Wong was on his hands and knees in his driveway when Ryan poured a bag of rice over his head. I wanted to help, especially after Ryan fired celebratory rounds. I could have sauntered over with Super Shorty.

But I would have had to battle Ryan's punks, most with guns of their own.

Ryan gets out. The chrome handle of his gun protrudes from the waistband of his jeans. His face is crusted with the fuzz of a wannabe beard. He was a senior when RBV closed. "Mister Big Nose," he smirks, striding over. "Where you heading?"

I say nothing.

Ryan plucks up a metal ADT home security sign and flings it like a Frisbee. He looks past me at Evo. She's got Sudzy in a death grip. I know Ryan has a crush because I've seen him peeping when Evo's out gardening. "Brought the cat," Ryan says.

"Cats dig the road," I answer. My fingers rest on Super Shorty's stock in the door's compartment.

"Clearing out for good?" Ryan asks.

"Just camping."

"Where?"

"Julian."

He smacks his lips. "Yum," he goes, "apple pie. Bring me back one?"

"Sure thing. Now let us pass."

He looks over at the F-150.

I see heads in the backseat. I'll bet they all have guns.

"In case you haven't heard, Big Nose," Ryan tells me, "we have a toll now."

"How much?" Evo asks.

"Five gold ounces."

I drum the wheel. "You a bad ass, Ryan?"

He pulls his gun—a semi-automatic with a long barrel. "I'm sick of your fucking bullshit, man."

"Will you take sterling?" asks Evo.

"Sterling what?"

"Silver spoons, from Europe."

"No sale."

"Don't be too hasty," I go. "One's got Marie Antoinette in the bowl."

"Who the fuck's she?" Ryan asks, lowering his gun.

"The ultimate party girl," Evo replies.

"Know too many skanks as it is."

"Evo," I say, "gimme the pouch."

"E-vo," Ryan echoes. "What a bitchin' name."

Evo pops the glove box and pulls out the leather pouch. She jiggles it and the silver clinks.

I snatch Super Shorty and stick it in Ryan's face. "Drop it," I go, "right where you stand."

"Your stick's not even loaded, Big Nose."

"My hubby never bluffs," Evo says.

Ryan's gun thuds on the asphalt.

I ease out with Super Shorty. "Now gimme something, Ryan."

"Say what?"

"My time's worth something, chewing the fat with a joker like you."

I follow him to the Ford. He yanks open the driver's door and the aroma of pot wafts out. The boys in back say nothing. Ryan pulls out a black duffel bag.

"Toss it and walk away," I tell him.

"You can't have it all."

"Oh, yes, I can."

"Or what?"

I raise Super Shorty and nestle his chest in the sights. I imagine the kick and buckshot flying.

Ryan underhands the duffel toward me. "You die, Big Nose," he says, "someday, you die."

I pick up his gun, cock it, and fire into his radiator—the bullet tears open the grill and antifreeze spurts like a geyser.

"Shit-ski!" goes Ryan.

The boys scramble out through the tailgate door. I fire again, this time point blank at a front tire. I hear a wicked gasp as it flattens. I toss the gun over Dr. Wong's fence and pass the duffel to Evo. I get in Rovy and slip Super Shorty back in my door.

Ryan's got both hands on his radiator. Antifreeze spurts between his fingers.

I drive over the curb and roll across his front lawn.

"You're dead, Big Nose!"

I reach Crystal Ridge, hang a right on Longhorn, and go left on Shadowridge. I wonder how many of the miles between us and Crestline will be a struggle. "Would you have shot him?" Evo asks.

"Maybe."

"Scaring's one thing, Tony. Shooting's another."

"Ryan pulled first."

"He was showing off."

"Right," I tell her.

Between you and me, I would have shot. I've never killed before but I will if it means protecting us. I reach for Sudzy and stroke fur that feels like mink. "What's in that duffel?" I ask.

THE COAST

EVO DIGS through the bag. She finds wallets, garage door openers, a jade bracelet, silver Pan American bars sealed in plastic, gold coins, rubber banded wads of cash, clove cigarettes, bullets, engraved ivory tusks, and a glass jar filled with a brown substance.

Evo spins open the lid. "Score," she gleams, "shroomies!"

We reach a strip mall. Skateboarders leap over pizza box hurdles. A girl tags a window. A gang strips a Mercedes. Beads of glass from broken windshields sparkle in the lot.

I take a dirt road and pull over at the pond. "Solo mission," I tell Evo, opening the cargo door. I grab the cooler and head down the bank. Mud hens, geese, seagulls, and ducks swarm me. I wave them off. I open the cooler, pull out the turts, and place them on the mud. "Goodbye, Heebie," I mumble, "fun times ahead, Jeebie."

They sit there, heads and legs tucked inside their shells. "Get going," I grouch. Jeebie sticks out her head. Heebie takes off—he scrambles over the mud and enters the pond. A goose pecks at his shell. I carry Jeebie and place her at the edge of the water. A mud hen screeches. Jeebie darts in and joins Heebie near a clump of moss. They tread water as ducklings glide by. Heebie dives. Jeebie heads for the pampas. Summer's coming, and I know they'll survive but I'm mad at myself for letting them go. They could outlive me, but who knows how polluted this pond might get. A drought would make it disappear. I hear footsteps. Evo takes my hand. I see turts stacked like pancakes next to a fern. "Sudzy okay?" I ask.

"The princess is curled up on your sweater."

I smile but feel empty inside. I feel bad losing my turtles after years of being together. Funny how the people and creatures I care about always seem to leave, just when I'm starting to really love them.

*　　　*　　　*

I backtrack to Shadowridge Drive and pass the RBV stadium. Tweens huddle under a coral tree. Two men take turns prying open a fire hydrant with a wrench. I flash back to my parents. Dadio was NYFD and died in the 9-11 disaster. Mom passed a year later from a broken heart. I hit the play button. The speakers crank out Social Distortion's "Reach for the Sky." Evo begs to see the water of the Pacific once more before heading for high ground. "Lake in Crestline," I remind her.

"The Crestline Puddle," she goes.

"Water's water."

"You don't understand. I want to look across miles of water and feel like I'm at the edge of the old world and the start of the new."

Hope is what Evo wants. She's right about that lake in

Crestline. But it's clean with a sandy beach and plenty of sun. We'll stay at the cabin until order's restored in San Diego.

"Coast could be dangerous," I grumble.

"Beach folk are mellow, Tony."

I remember beachcombing in Carlsbad with Evo on Valentine's Day. The sky was lavender. It felt like a dream, with the waves crashing, dolphins offshore, and being with the woman I love. Evo wanted to forget about us buying inland. Instead, she ached to rent a beach house so she could fall asleep to the sound of the surf every night.

The traffic lights are out on Melrose Drive. Most drivers fly through intersections. I do a California stop and nearly hit a merging Prius. We reach the 78 on-ramp and head west. The yellow blossoms of wild mustard cover the freeway's shoulders. Traffic is mostly hybrids and electrics. SUVs are parked in the emergency lane. A red Trans Am blows by. "Gas hog," I grumble. But I should talk. Rovy gets 20 mpg max. Thank god we've got a full tank and a reserve 40 in cargo.

I take the Vista Way off-ramp and go south on a two-laner with an ocean view. Tiki faces are carved in the trunks of palms. The asphalt has wicked cracks and I negotiate an obstacle course of shattered fiberglass, loose dogs, and darting kids. Locals puff on hookahs. A kid loses his balloon and cries as it flies over the Outer Limits Smoke Shop. Tramps wiggle cardboard signs: WORK FOR FOOD, GUNS 4 GOLD, and FRESH WATER. Shopping carts are stuffed with wetsuits, swim fins, boogie boards, and coolers. I crank the wheel and barely miss a hippie riding a Vespa. I beeline for Carlsbad. Crows gobble down strings of red meat in the median. The old WELCOME TO CARLSBAD sign now reads, COME TO BAD. PCH cuts through a lagoon and we pass a girl skimming the tea-colored surface with a net. Guards smoke on the steps of the Carlsbad By the Sea retirement home. We slip through rows of white stucco barracks, where boys in military blues stand around a pole flying the flag at half-mast.

I park at St. Michael's Church.

"Beach?" Evo suggests.

"That's what you want, right?"

"I'll worry about Sudzy."

"Confine the princess to her carrier."

"How long?"

"An hour."

"Let's make it half-an-hour."

"You got it, Babe."

Evo passes me Sudzy. She pours cat sand in a shoebox and places it on the floor. Sudzy kicks out of my arms and lands on the dash. She howls like a banshee when I grab her.

"Crazy Russian Blue," I tell Evo.

"You're the one feeding her under the table."

"You sneak her organic cream."

"That makes her fur shine," Evo claims.

We crack the windows and head for the parish courtyard. A man in diapers jerks by on a walker. We reach the courtyard, where volunteers pass bottled water and boxes hand-to-hand into the Church. A canopy booth and table is outside the Community Room. Parishioners mill around the booth munching off paper plates. A lady in a blue frock stirs greens in a glass bowl with wooden spoons.

"What's in there?" Evo asks.

"Cacti, kelp, medallions of ice plant."

"Talk about roughage," I mutter.

The lady gives me the stink eye. "Better full and happy than empty and angry," she responds, grabbing a yellow mustard bottle. She squirts an oily sauce into the bowl and tosses it vigorously.

"What's your dressing?" Evo presses.

"Limes. Fresh-ground pepper. Olive oil."

"Soup?"

"Cream of squash, five sharp."

"Any cat food?" I joke.

"Rats in the thrift shop attic."

I grab Evo's hand and tug her away. We stroll past the Carlsbad

Inn. A boy with dreadlocks darts out of the hotel with a flat screen. A girl exits clutching a brass dolphin. We amble down Ocean Street. The stop sign's riddled with holes. A tween hops up on a truck's bumper and thrusts his dirk at the sky. The old fence across from the Church has been knocked down, and rollerbladers race along Ocean Street.

"Go, Dawg Boy!" a man cheers the racers.

"Nobody beats Elvis," a toothless woman brags.

We take the public stairs. Hillside cane rustles in the breeze, and underwear swings on a bungee cord stretched between stalks. Surfboards and kayaks are piled on a flat spot, and a man stands on a boulder swinging nunchucks.

We reach the beach. The Pacific is as flat and reflective as aluminum foil. Surfers float the shiny sea. One stands on his board and paddles through the oily beds of kelp. Tents and cinder block shanties cover acres of sand on either side of the stairway. We weave through an encampment that seems more permanent than temporary. A man loads his carbine. His woman cooks on a rusty stove. Babies are everywhere. We reach a shore lined with rods. I flash to a Coney Island boat show Dadio took me to, one where I tried hooking goldfish in a giant blue tub. I could only use bread for bait and the fish swam by looking bored.

"What's biting?" I ask a man in a Red Sox shirt.

"Surf perch and snapper," he grunts, "sometimes a ray."

"What's your favorite?"

"Anything I can sink my teeth into," he chuckles. "Stingray's best in soy sauce. Had some kid gobble a jellyfish."

"Yucko," Evo frowns.

"If I was starving," he tells us, "I'd eat rubber. Know what they call this place?"

"What?" I ask.

"Funky Town." He introduces himself as Fred, a former native of Worcester, Massachusetts. I don't know why, but Fred tells us his great grandfather resided at the Worcester Insane Asylum until the day he died.

Evo and I head north along the shore. The waves spew up butts, plastic bottles, and tiny red crabs. Boys and girls gather the crabs and drop them in plastic buckets. A blue Olds missing its hood chugs by. It's strange returning to the beach where I first met Evo, a place once filled with romance and magic. The sun drops on the sooty horizon. A surfer paddles toward a drifting yacht.

"Seen enough water?" I ask Evo.

"I hate it here."

We head back to the stairs. Fire rings flash to life. A toddler fills a box with sand. Fred offers us a place at his camp so we sit beside his tiny fire. He hands us sardines impaled on bamboo slivers. "Cook 'em crisp," he says.

Evo crinkles her nose. "What about bones?"

"No worries. Bones snap like potato chips."

I stick my sardine in. The fins burn and the skin crinkles. I carry the fish to my mouth, blow it cool, and chomp the head. "Tasty," I say.

Evo sticks in her sardine. "By the way," she goes, "where's my Buddha?"

"Sorry, Babe. No room at the inn."

"Aloha, good karma."

We finish the sardines. The sun sneaks below the ocean, turning the sky a sullen brown. I check out Oceanside Pier to the north. An oil tanker is grounded in the shallows. *Boom-ah-boom-boom-boom* echoes along the cliffs.

"Funky Town music," Fred says.

I elbow Evo. "Ready for Crestline?"

"Ready," she replies.

THE GOOD SAMARITAN

WE CLIMB and descend hills on the 15. The sun is below the northern mountains and shadows stretch over the lanes. A man is trying to pry open a Safeway cargo door with a crow bar. This freeway's a mess of abandoned rigs, massive trucks, cement mixers, and bulldozers. A crane chained to a steel trailer looks like an alien insect with the pink light of sunset reflecting off its boom.

"Careful!" goes Evo.

I swerve and narrowly miss a coyote.

I wonder about this new world, one where it doesn't matter what you did or didn't do. What matters is what you do now. I crest a hill and pick up speed on the descent. An off-road fire flickers and hobos crowd the flames.

*   *   *

We pass Rainbow and make the Temecula checkpoint at twilight. Floodlights glare from metal poles. No border guards. No vehicles with sweating passengers waiting to be questioned. A man on a car's roof waves a MERCY sign. A woman in a red dress leans against the checkpoint office door.

"Mercy?" I ask Evo.

"Buddha would."

I pull up behind a blue Maverick and tap Super Shorty's stock.

The man slides off the roof and tosses the sign. He's wearing a yellow bowling shirt, glittering green pants, and glasses. His blond hair is slicked sideways. He makes his way over to my side.

I power my window down.

"Son," he whimpers through thin lips, "Molly's run dry. We need gas, at least two gallons to reach Riverside. We coasted in neutral and this is how far she took me and Mommy."

"Will two gallons do it?" I ask.

"Yes." He reaches for his oxblood shoe and pulls out a coin. "Got gold on me."

I kill the engine. I figure he's heading to a relative's home, maybe a son or a daughter. "No gold," I tell him. "No charge."

"Now, son, that would hardly be fair."

"I'll take nada."

"Mommy," he calls, "did you hear that?"

"Hear what, Daddy?"

"Gas! Gallons, delivered by the generous hands of the Lord."

"Bet that boy's from Oklahoma," she chortles.

The breeze lifts Daddy's hair like a lid, revealing a bald spot. He pats it back down. "Son," he croons, "let us pay. Me and Mommy don't mind giving some for your Christian kindness."

I pluck Rovy's keys, slide them in my pocket, and get out. I keep my lights on. I stand inside a white square painted on the cement, one of the boxes guards made suspected illegals cower in during interrogations. The floodlights make me feel as though I'm in a stadium during a night game.

"You know me," I tell Daddy. "I'm the Good Samaritan."

"Well, Lordy me," he claps. "Mommy, we have us a man of The Bible, a true practitioner of the Good Book."

Mommy waddles over, clutching a Foster's Lager. Her eyes are glassy and her cheeks are caked with rouge. "I know that boy's from Oklahoma."

Daddy holds up his hand. "Time for man talk," he tells Mommy. "Go visit the missus."

"Finishing my brew first, Ahab."

"Do as you please, Mommy."

I ease around Rovy. That can't be his real name, I think. Wasn't Ahab that crazy captain who harpooned the white whale? I run a hand over my ribcage and feel the Beretta. I pop the cargo door, grab the can with the built-in funnel, and head over to Molly. I spin open her fuel cap, stick the funnel in, and tilt. The premium smells good. I love the sound of gas gurgling in. I gaze into Molly's wing mirror and see Evo sitting in Rovy. I hear a splashing sound—gas pours out of Molly.

Daddy hustles over. "Something wrong?"

"Molly had gas."

"Well, I'll be a monkey's uncle. Fuel isn't her problem, now is it?"

I pull out the funnel and put the can down. Something jams against the small of my back.

"If you value your health, son, you won't turn around."

"Is that your finger, Daddy?"

"Not a chance. This is a Colt 45. Killed many a sinner already, and ready to do my bidding again. You'd last five minutes, rolling around bleeding like a stuck pig. Your lady would be next. No heroics, son. On your knees, like you're praying for salvation in the good Lord's House."

I kneel in a puddle of gas. He sticks the barrel against my head. I want to reach for the Beretta. I gaze into the night sky. I don't see any stars because of the glaring floodlights.

"Son," says Daddy, "I'll be needing those keys, so me and Mommy can mosey on down the road. Molly's dead but you're welcome to her, full tank and all. You could tinker a bit, bring her back to life, the way Jesus raised Lazarus."

That sounds comforting. But why would Daddy give me the

chance to revive Molly and hunt him down? He's going to kill me. He'll kill Evo too. Does she know what's happening? I hear scraping. I spot a short barrel inching out from under Rovy's front bumper.

"Let's forget all this," I tell Daddy, "before anyone gets hurt. I forgive you, you accept my forgiveness, we shake on it, and both walk away better people."

Daddy chuckles. "Son, I give you credit for trying, but you're in a helluva position to negotiate. Reach in your pocket and pull out your keys nice and slow. Dangle them over your head. No tricks now."

I fish out the keys and hold them high.

Daddy snatches them.

A *boom* rocks the checkpoint and makes the floodlights rattle.

"Lord Almighty!" goes Mommy.

I get up and spin around. Daddy's wriggling without a shoe. His revolver's on the blacktop and he's squirming toward it. I beat him over, pick up the Colt, and take aim.

"Mercy, son!"

Evo appears, cradling Super Shorty.

"Where's Mommy?" I ask.

"Duck taped."

I spot a shoe across the median. The sock on Daddy's foot is soaked with blood. His pants smolder from shot but he's still clutching my keys.

I pull the hammer. "Gimme the keys, Daddy."

He throws them—they fly and land in a white square.

"Blast him if he moves," I tell Evo.

"With pleasure."

I get the keys.

"Please," Daddy begs, "me and Mommy, we're God-fearing folks. Take what you want, only let us live to do the Lord's work."

"Satan's work is more like it," Evo replies.

I go to one knee and hold the .45's barrel against his temple. The lid of his hair is plastered back and his bald spot glows like a full moon. "We're talking lights out, Daddy," I go, "unless you swear to never harm a stranger again."

"I swear to God!"

I toss the Colt. It skids over the interstate and ends up in the scrub.

Mommy's in Molly's backseat and Evo cuts her free with a Swiss Army knife. We let Mommy go and she slippers toward Daddy. "That boy's not from Oklahoma," she says.

"Get Daddy's shoe!"

Mommy heads out to the median. She puts her hands of her hips. "Where the fuck is it?"

Evo and I get back in Rovy.

She passes me Super Shorty. "Bless me, Father," she says, "for I have sinned."

"Have you told an untruth, child?" I ask.

"I hunted with Knute. Someone had to keep him company."

"Didn't your brothers hunt?"

"They were too busy skiing and chasing girls."

I wedge Super Shorty back in my door. "Wha'd you shoot?"

"Elk. Bucks only."

"You look like an elk girl. I figured you knew something the way you handled the shotgun."

"Promise one thing, Tone."

"Name it."

"No more Good Samaritan."

I fire up the engine. "What about karma?"

"Forget karma for now," Evo says, "at least until we reach that cabin."

CRESTLINE OR BUST

I CAN SEE for miles ahead using my high beams. Hills give way to long lean stretches of freeway. Stars glimmer above the San Bernardino Mountains. Crestline's up there somewhere. I can tell Evo's rattled by the way she clutches Sudzy. Daddy sure surprised us.

A man beside an overturned truck tries flagging us down but I don't stop. We scorch through Sun City, Perris, and Moreno Valley. Cars rarely pass going south. I'm glad we're leaving the lowlands and coast. I'm tired yet eager to begin the ascent to the cabin.

*   *   *

We're on the 215 that will take us to Crestline. I see blue and red lights flashing at the merger. A line of vehicles a mile long waits for fire trucks and squad cars to move. I idle behind a gray GMC truck and watch helicopters buzz the foothills. Sudzy cries.

"The princess okay?" I ask.

"She's hungry," Evo says.

"Salmon treat?"

Evo unzips her fanny pack and slips out a few kibbles.

Sudzy's crunching sound makes me smile.

"Is there another way, Tone?"

"We have to reach the 10. If that's blocked we'd need to off-road it up these mountains."

"Could we do it?"

"I guess. But we can't ignore the Hill People."

"Hill People?"

"Tell you later," I mutter. The Hill People Bulletin was the last warning before the radio died. They were a Wrightwood clan determined to keep outsiders away. But they ran out of food and scoured the high country for any meat they could find. The bulletin went out the day a ranger found a pot of human stew simmering in a Wrightwood cauldron.

Boots *clumpity-clump* and soldiers shout orders. They're turning vehicles back.

The GMC truck nearly clips us reversing. The driver scoots to the shoulder and descends the embankment. The GMC reaches the desert floor and rumbles north. Hummers converge like a pack of scorpions. The driver keeps going. Jeeps give chase. A helicopter lights up the truck. I hear gunfire and the GMC's engulfed in a swirl of dust.

A soldier with an M-16 approaches us.

"How's the 215, soldier?" I ask.

"Jack-knifed big rig," he answers. "There's no way up these mountains."

"Can't you tow the rig?"

He bangs our fender with the M-16's butt. "Sir, you need to go back."

I crank the wheel and follow a hoard heading south on the 15. I can't return to Portico. I pull over and study the wing mirrors. No soldiers in sight. "Better put Sudzy in the carrier," I tell Evo, "we're in for a bumpy ride."

"What's your plan?" she asks.

"Sneak across the desert till we reach the 60."

"They'll come for us."

I turn the headlights off. The lights from the roadblock ignite 100 yards of open desert. We'd be hard to spot if Rovy makes it to the shadows beyond those 100 yards. "That GMC was heading north," I tell Evo. "The southeast's safe."

"How safe?"

"Safer than off-roading to Crestline."

"And our destination?"

"Dave's."

"Gay Dave?"

"The one and only."

"No water in the Mojave, Tone."

"Dave's gotta spring."

"He's still there?"

"Dave sunk every dime into Pinyon Crest. Where else would he go?"

Evo squeezes Sudzy into her carrier and places it on the floor mat. "Hell," she mutters. "Just go for it."

I sneak to the shoulder. I shift to 4WD and creep down the embankment—we tilt at 45 degrees. Rovy moans. We level out on the desert floor, and I hit the pedal. We fly over a wash, plow through scrub, and crush a yucca. I reach the shadows. A rim scuffs a ledge. I blast through cacti, swerve to avoid a boulder, and kick up tumbleweeds. I ease up on the pedal and see stars above an eastern mountain range. Those must be the San Gabriels. If we hit Highway 60 we'll be in good shape.

I remember Dave bartending for me after teaching all day. Everyone called him "Gay Dave." He didn't mind. He transformed a V-bottomed junker into a pirate ship complete with sails, mast, and water cannons. He named her *Miss Avalon*. Families loved sailing with him around Mission Bay and San Diego Harbor. He sold *Miss Avalon* and moved to Pinyon Crest two years ago with Justin, the first mate on the ship. But Justin met a model in Palm Springs and they hiked off into the sunset, leaving Dave alone in a pup tent. I think part of Dave was lonely, but the other part craved solitude. He already owned the land so he built a sustainable ranch in the Mojave. I locked his coordinates into my GPS years ago, after promising a visit.

"Let's GPS it," I tell Evo.

She plucks the GPS out of the console and plugs it into the slot for the lighter. The GPS lady doesn't speak. Even with the flashing screen making satellite contact, she can't find us in the desert.

"Where does she think we are?" I ask.

"Colorado."

I go southeast, relying on the rear-view mirror's digital compass. The ride's smooth, although we go airborne when we fly off a mini-gulch at the edge of the plain. Sudzy doesn't cry. I shoot the gap between Box Springs Mountain to the west and the Norton Younglove Reserve foothills to the east. I jam the moon roof open—the aroma of sage drifts in. Stars crowd the sky.

"Eyes on the road," Evo scolds.

"What road, Babe?"

I wonder about life in distant galaxies. Dave swore there was a parallel universe right here on Earth. He claimed he heard parallel beings gabbing whenever he switched on his fan. He said they played music but it was impossible to understand them. "What kind of music?" I asked.

"Similar to Rachmaninoff," he answered. Dave told me to put a floor fan on high and listen to the spinning blades. That guy's kooky as hell, but he's certainly not boring.

"Do you believe in a parallel universe?" I ask Evo.

"Not that again. Hungry?"

"Starving."

"Power bar?"

"Snickers."

"Sugar addict."

"Guilty as charged."

She pulls a bar from her fanny pack, unwraps it, and sticks an end in my mouth.

We drop into a tunnel-like wash and I turn on the headlights. I brake at a rise that seems unnatural, one with a cement lip fringing the top. "Hello, 60," I smile, "you beautiful thing."

"Can we make it, Tone?"

"Let's find out." I shift to second, slam the pedal, and the rear tires squeal. We hit loose rocks going up and the fronts lose traction. The chassis gets caught on the lip. I downshift to first and the rears dig in. We go over the lip and hit asphalt. I shift to two-wheel. We follow Highway 60 until we reach the 10 and cut through Beaumont. The cherry orchards give off a sweet, rose-like aroma.

*   *   *

We arrive at Owl, a tiny town with cobbled streets. The rolling tires sound like heartbeats. We reach old wooden storefronts that look like they belong to the Wild West. The stores are all closed. We pass Antique Heaven, Thrifty Drugs, Coyote Café, and Harvey's Feed. Harvey's has a petting zoo out back. A glowing sign on the edge of town catches my attention.

"Hola, Texaco," I say.

I pull up to a pump. A generator hums in the garage and a man wearing a yellow jumpsuit shuffles toward me. He's holding a breaker bar. "No credit," he goes, "and no greenbacks."

I climb out. "Don't have that," I tell him.

"Whatcha tradin' with?"

"Barbra Streisand CDs."

"No, for chrissakes."

"Silver?"

He reaches Rovy and inches closer, his cowboy boots squeaking. ROY is on a nametag stitched above his breast pocket. "Who's your maker?" he asks.

"Northwest Territorial Mint, outta Washington."

"Two ounces a gallon," Roy mumbles. "Won't take less."

"Deal."

"Start pumpin'."

I shove in the nozzle and listen to the premium gurgle. I breathe deeply, enjoying the smell of gas. Roy's stance is stiff, like a cowboy ready to draw. I spot a bulge in the jumpsuit beneath the tag.

"Killin' out there?" Roy asks me.

"Not so far."

"Safe as Mizzou here."

There's a kid out by a cherry tree at the edge of the lot. He swings an ax and the blade bounces off the trunk. "Your boy?" I ask Roy.

"No. That's Dim-bulb Carter. His old man gave 'im that ax before hightailin' it for Vegas. Carter drinks ditch water and eats road kill."

"No mother?"

"Ma lives in yonder dog house," he hiccups, pointing toward Banning. "Good mile past that orchard."

I keep pumping.

Roy parks his breaker bar on my hood. "Sorry to be so ornery," he says. "City slicker gives me Year of the Pig. Damn thing's clad, not silver all the way through. Got in a heapa shit with Mister Texaco."

"Chinese silver's tricky," I say.

Roy snatches the breaker bar. "Say, how you like this here Rover?"

"Love her. But something's always leaking."

"Ain't a Rover if she don't leak."

The nozzle clicks off and Roy studies the pump's dial. "That'll be 34 ounces, mister," he goes, holding out his hand.

"Bullion time," I call.

Evo gets out with the duffel bag, zips it open, and hands him the bars.

Roy fondles them with greasy fingers. He stacks the bullion on the lid of a garbage can between pumps. He counts them out loud and counts again.

Evo does the Warrior pose and points east. "Look, Tony."

I look over the dark land—flames from the desert shoot into the sky. It's beautiful but ominous at the same time.

"Headin' east?" Roy asks.

"Palm Springs," I reply.

"Wouldn't go, not if I was you."

"No?"

He shakes his head. "Camp in Owl, till things blow over. Welcome to stake a claim in town, maybe hole up at Harvey's.

Plenty of cherries, and I know how to get water."

I turn to Evo. The eastern flames catch the highlights in her hair. "Into the belly of the beast?" I ask.

She holds out her hands. "Deliver me to Dave's."

HELL SPRINGS

THE DATE PALMS are fireballs. Fire engulfs the Palm Springs Hilton and explosions rock the hotel. We pass Racquet Club West, Historic Tennis Club, and Movie Colony. These burbs have 3-story mansions with garish gates, brick driveways, and security hedges. A family huddles on their lawn as looters plunder. A Porsche screams down Palm Canyon Drive as teens roam Araby Cove with garbage bags slung over their shoulders. I zip around a wheelchair, narrowly miss a leather couch, and sideswipe a flat screen. A front tire hits a glass chandelier, cracking it.

Evo grimaces. "Lead crystal."

Tweens stand beside a coral tree guzzling from decanters. They laugh watching a skinhead chainsaw through a front door.

"Forgot to pill Sudzy," I confess.

"Pull over, Tone."

"Okay. But somewhere safe."

Boys on the sidewalk duel with torches. Another fires a derringer. It's pandemonium, with crazies running back and forth across Palm Canyon while flames leap home to home. It feels as though the entire world's on fire. I imagine fleeing from one burning city to the next, our child never knowing the peace and comfort of someplace safe. Webs of colored light strobe a cul-de-sac. Kids gather around a jacked-up Dodge Ram and pump fists to a techno version of "Smells Like Teen Spirit."

"Psytrance party," Evo tells me.

"You've been to one?" I ask.

"Lady Gaga tranced out the Ghost Bar."

I pull over. A DJ wearing black jeans and black elbow pads stands in the Ram's bed. A small keyboard with a mic dangles off a strap around his neck. He fingers the keys and wails with a raspy voice. The odor in the air reminds me of the desert. But not this desert. "What's that smell?" I ask Evo.

"Patchouli."

Group dance begins. Some link arms and spiral around the truck. Then comes more fist pumping as the DJ's amplified voice joins the *crackle-pop* of burning trees and mansions. A boy wears the American flag like a cape. A girl bangs a bongo. Here is the celebration of a city being reduced to ashes. Bright eyes flash victory. These teens have no fear of losing everything because it all belonged to their parents anyway. Young lives swell with meaning in Palm Springs as the new world burns up the old.

I take off and drive miles before pulling over again. I keep the engine running and switch on the interior lights. A woman in a leg cast crutches by. Evo hands me latex gloves and the bottle of cancer pills. She pries open Sudzy's mouth—I slip a pill behind her tongue.

"Good girl," coos Evo.

I hate pilling. The princess lost her whiskers that first month. But her fur's fine. Dr. Grady told us we'd extend Sudzy's life a year and that was five months ago. I run my hand down her back and feel her spine. Whenever I think she's fading, Sudzy rallies. She was chasing lizards last week and her purr's strong. I snap off the latex gloves and stuff them in a plastic bag. There's a knock on my window. A hooded man is holding up a necklace.

"No," Evo tells me.

I power the window down.

"Emeralds," he snorts, "the real deal."

"How much?"

"Got go-juice for my buggy?"

I study the gems. "They look like glass, bro."

He darts in front and dangles the necklace in my headlights. The stones sparkle a clear green.

"Wow," I go.

"Don't give him gas," Evo says, sticking Sudzy back in her carrier.

The man returns to my window. "Guaranteed," he promises, "from Paris Hilton's villa. Five gallons and you own it."

"Where's Paris?" Evo asks.

"Bottom of the pool."

"Three gallons," I offer.

"Four."

"Deal," I say, shaking his hand.

*   *   *

We leave Palm Springs four gallons lighter but with an emerald necklace hanging off the rear-view mirror. Evo won't touch it. The emeralds catch flashes of fire and glow a green that reminds me of jungles. I tell Evo the necklace will make up for me not getting her an engagement ring.

"Wonder what Paris did with those emeralds," Evo grouses.

"Love beads?" I joke.

"Ew, sick."

"I could drop it in boiling water to kill the germs."

"Boil away," goes Evo, "but I'll wear nothing that Paris touched."

*   *   *

We hit a Palm Desert strip mall. Lights ignite stacks of guns, hardware, and tools in the parking lot. A man in a madras prowls the roof of Burger King. "Rifles, Aisle Four," he says through a megaphone, "chainsaws, Aisle Six."

Our GPS finds us. The GPS lady guides us through an inferno of torched cars to the Palms to Pines Highway. I turn south. The GPS says we're twenty miles from Dave's. He emailed photos of a giant Joshua tree marking his turnoff but I know the GPS won't find that tree.

The highway is a two-laner that cuts through a pass between mountains dotted with boulders. Clusters of palm trees sprout on the roadside. I go high beam. We tackle an incline that becomes a nightmare of hairpins. I misjudge one—the tires on Evo's side crush a baby palm. "Jesus," I mutter, swinging the wheel.

We finally break free of the hairpins. The road straightens. Our tires hum over the asphalt and Evo plops Sudzy on her lap. Pines replace the cacti and sagebrush. Mesas, mountains with their tops sheared off, hunch in the south. Three coyotes watch us pass, their eyes glowing in the lights. I spot Andromeda above the mesas, not far from Scorpio. The stars make the Mojave safe because these constellations are old friends. I've always loved the night sky, ever since Dadio gave me a telescope for Christmas. He loved gazing at the rings of Saturn and the red glow of Mars.

Evo rolls up a blanket and uses it like a pillow against her window. Sudzy snores on her lap. All this driving can't be good for the princess or our baby. I feel lousy about Crestline, but have faith in Pinyon Crest. Dave's compound is nestled in a valley fed by mountain streams. It should be safe.

Something dark looms ahead. I ease up on the pedal. A massive body reaches gnarled arms over the road. I close in and realize they're not arms at all but branches. It's the Joshua tree. The lower trunk is a mass of nubs where branches broke off. I turn onto a road framed by pinyons. Our tires swirl through gravel.

"Turn right," goes the GPS lady.

I spin the wheel and see a mountain's silhouette. It rises toward Aries and blocks out half the sky.

"Turn left," instructs the lady.

I take a narrow road carpeted with spongy ice plant. Oranges glisten on trees. The blossoms smell tangy. I stop at an ivy gate, where a Buddha squats in the lotus position on its crest. A pine NAMASTE plaque hangs off a chain around the Buddha's neck.

"Arrived at destination," says the GPS lady.

"Bingo!" I say.

Evo stirs. She stretches and strokes Sudzy. "Where are we, Tone?"

"Nirvana."

NIRVANA

EVO SLEEPS in my arms. Her lips part and her tongue moves as if she's talking in a dream. I notice that sexy space between her front teeth. "Hottie," I whisper. Her chest rises and falls. I like how her hair always seems to stay in place. Her eyelashes quiver. "Pass on the dream," Dadio told me, "you'll forever be chasing it." I didn't pass. Her breasts, the size of mangoes, feel good against my chest. I run my fingers over her bare shoulders and down her arm. Nothing calms me more than being with my woman like this. The upside to Cali imploding is having more time with her. I was coming home at three a.m. after closing the bar to find Evo asleep on the couch with the flat screen blaring. She said I was job co-dependent, the way Mom told Dadio he was married to the NYFD.

We're in Dave's guesthouse, a geodesic dome separated from the main casita by a garden. I smell cilantro. Light from the ceiling's pentagon window plays on our aqua sheets. The polar white trunks of eucalyptus shimmer beyond the glass. Sudzy snores on my wool sweater at the bottom of the bed. I wedge my toes under the princess. She continues snoring, despite the sound of pecking at the front door.

Knuckles *tap-tap-tap*.

I grab my boxer's and tug them over my hips.

"Decent?" comes a voice.

"Oui, monsieur," I answer, "entrez."

The door opens and a man stands at the entrance. He looks down sheepishly, like a child who walked in on his parents. He's wiry with a pointy chin and black goatee. "Shoo, shoo, shoo," he says, waving away chickens. He looks stylish in a white crew tee, pineapple shorts, and moccasins. He could be the host of a game show giving away trips to the tropics. "The Dynamic Duo," he greets us. "Sleep good?"

"Like the dead, Dave," I answer. "Hot out?"

"92 in the shade."

"Cool in here."

He winks. "Designed it that way, Tony."

A hoard of feathered creatures gathers around Dave. Hens peck at his pants. Chicks scurry around his moccasins. A rooster sticks his head in and offers a half-crow. Sudzy quits snoring. Dave tosses kernels of corn and the horde scampers off.

Evo's eyes open. "Hi, Daver."

"Hey, Vegas," he answers. "Want breakfast?"

She plucks a black bra off her nightstand and snaps it on. "Buffet style, I presume?"

"Beats the Golden Nugget," Dave smiles, his blue eyes flashing.

He wheels in a wooden cart with a breakfast bar attached. Sudzy hisses and retreats to the pillow behind me. One of the wheels catches, and the cart does a 180 on the carpet. "For the luva Pete," Dave groans. He backs up until the wheel frees.

Sudzy leaps off the bed and slips under my nightstand.

"Scoot," Dave tells us.

We squirm to the edge and dangle our legs down. It feels like we're brats getting the royal treatment from a doting uncle, one that doesn't mind seeing us semi-nude. Dave wheels the cart over and the breakfast bar becomes our table. He swings open the side compartments. "Vegan omelets," he announces, "fresh eggs, zucchini, goat cheese, sun-dried tomatoes, and the whole shebang garnished with slivers of pinyon nut."

Evo waves her hand. "Vegan freak right here."

"Got sausage?" I ask.

Dave crosses his arms. "Not on this ranch, cowboy. Took the liberty of making scrambled for your Russian Blue."

"Cool beans," Evo goes.

Dave pulls out a bowl and places it beside my nightstand. "Added a fillet of tilapia."

Sudzy's head appears and I hear sniffing. She slinks out and samples Dave's offering.

"The princess is lucky to get canned tuna from me," I confess.

"Tight wad," Dave snaps. He aims a camera and takes a Polaroid of us in bed. "Here it comes," he says, watching it develop.

"Any good?" asks Evo.

"You're a fox, Vegas. But who's that beast beside you?"

*   *   *

After breakfast, I pull on my cargo pants, tank, and battered high-tops. Evo looks hot in her shredded cut-offs, white halter, and leopard sneakers. Her belly's lean and her buns look rock hard wrapped in denim. She puts on her khaki safari hat and flips the strap of my old canteen over her shoulder. The time to explore has arrived.

Dave leads us through a meadow of yellow, orange, and purple ice plant. Cosmo, his golden retriever, cools in the pond below. Dave tells us the stream feeding that pond is Nirvana's lifeblood. He whistles for his dog.

Cosmo looks up. He paddles through the lily pads, climbs onto the bank, and shakes off water. He runs through the meadow and joins us. We climb Turbine Hill. The heat's dry, and I hardly sweat. We reach a dozen cactus-green propellers, the *womp-ah-womp-womp* of their blades echoing off the arroyo. Dave says a generator on each turbine makes electricity when the blades turn and that underground cables store output in a tank that's like a giant battery.

"Enough wind?" I ask.

"Sundowners boost me at dusk."

"Where's storage?" Evo asks.

Dave points to an adjacent hill. "See that big purple steel thingy?"

I spot a purple tank that resembles a miniature reservoir. "Vivid."

"Paint sale," Dave admits, "at Home Despair."

Nirvana feels safe. There's no sign of anyone in the upper desert dominated by mountains, hardy pinions, and flat plateaus glinting orange-pink in the sun. The southern mesas have rust-red belts running through their middles. Sheep Mountain behind us curves around the edge of the ranch. I spot our geodome and Dave's peach casita, with a pool beside it. The Joshua tree stands like a guardian beside the black ribbon of highway.

We reach the canyon. Condors glide the arroyo walls, and the air smells clean. Evo holds out the canteen, and I take a swig. We pass turpentine bushes and enter a gulley of blue-green yucca. The yucca leaves remind me of swords.

Cosmo sticks his nose in a patch of manzanita between boulders.

"Rattlers out here, Dave?" I ask.

"Yes."

Cosmo snorts and paws. He digs and dirt flies.

"No, Cosmo," says Evo.

Cosmo keeps digging. A rabbit shoots out of the manzanita and

Cosmo gives chase through the yucca.

"Never caught one yet," Dave reassures us. He leads us out of the gulley and through a patch of orb-like cacti and umbrella succulents. We reach the canyon wall. Water trickles down the wall's face and collects in a basin.

"Source of my Nile," Dave tells us.

"Does it ever dry up?" asks Evo.

"Not during the two years I've been here. Taste it, Tony."

I kneel, cup the cold water, and carry it to my lips. It has a strong mineral taste. "Iron?" I ask, standing.

"A little. But you're tasting borax and copper."

Evo gets on her belly and squirms over to the basin. She drinks like a doe. Her long legs are already brown from the sun. Dave stares down at her. Evo empties the canteen and re-fills it.

"Hey," I go, "wasn't that once my canteen?"

"Don't use it," Evo teases, "you lose it."

We backtrack through the valley and gulley. I hear the echo of condor wings off the arroyo. We hike down Turbine Hill through the ice plant meadow and return to the dome. Dave says limestone walls keep the dome cool. The gunmetal gray roof is laid out in triangular sections. The sections fit into clusters of six, with pieces overlapping into adjacent clusters. The roof reminds me of a family of starfish.

The tour of the bottom acres begins. Dave shows us his pen of Nubian goats, a hen house stacked with wire cages, and the white trough that was once his tub. Cosmo laps the water. We reach a garden of corn, tomatoes, zucchini, and strawberries. Tiny propellers spin between the rows.

"Wind-powered irrigation?" I ask.

"Complete sustainability," he replies.

Evo plucks a strawberry. "Got herbs, Daver?"

"Enough for Herbes de Provence."

I yank a tomato. "What's that?"

"Let's see," he goes, tapping his chin. "For starters, I require savory, fennel, basil, thyme, and lavender, not to mention healthy doses of cilantro and rosemary."

"Lavender?" I ask, munching the tomato. "You making perfume?"

"You're an absolute cretin, Tony. Everyone knows flowers add incredible body to stews and sauces."

We continue our journey through an orchard of orange, lime, and avocado trees. I walk behind Evo because I love watching her buns flex and the way that canteen bounces seductively off her hip.

"Hey, Daver," goes Evo, "what kinda bird is that?"

"What bird?"

"On the orange tree. With yellow and black feathers."

Dave pulls a pair of opera glasses out of a pocket in his shorts. "Oriole."

"Orioles live in the east," I say.

Evo giggles. "That's the baseball team, Tone."

We meander through the trees, pick citrus, and arrive at Dave's house. His casita looks like a peach box with adobe walls, squared corners, and flat roof. It's built beside a pond fringed with reeds and pampas. Blue and silver fish swim the lotus water. There are even schools of polliwogs.

Evo crouches. "You have frogs?"

"Didn't hear them last night, Vegas?"

"I was unconscious upon arrival."

Dave laughs. "The Frog Concerto begins at dusk."

We continue down a river-stone path and enter a grotto guarded by a bronze Ganesh, the elephant god. Fern fronds shade a tropical garden of plumeria, torch ginger, and pink anthuriums. Dave ducks under a redwood archway with THE SEA OF CONSCIOUS CREATION carved in it. Spidery plants that live off air cling to the wood. Dave guides us through stalks of timber bamboo and we arrive at a turquoise pool shaped like a half-moon. A falls cascades down a wall of black stones into the pool.

"Salt water," Dave tells us. "The shell's granite."

"Why granite?" I ask.

"Granite's best for healing."

Evo tests the water. "Mighty warm, Daver."

"The temperature of blood. That's best for our bodies and the salt buoys us up like the ocean."

Whitebark pines crowd a bluff beyond the pool. Heat clouds shadow the mesas. "Lonely out here?" I ask.

"Extremely," goes Dave.

Evo plucks a bamboo leaf out of the pool. "Any neighbors?"

"Cody Tabeshaw, a half-blood Apache. He had a small horse ranch over that ridge to the south. I used to fill his water jugs."

"He split?" I ask.

"Cody had debts. Make enemies in the Mojave, and locals take the law into their own hands. Cody refused help when I offered it."

We stand poolside sharing an awkward silence. I sense a desperate kind of lonely in my friend, one that would make me worry leaving without him.

Dave stares at the pool. "Hey, Vegas," he goes, "Watsu at sunset?"

"I'm all yours, Daver."

"Is that like Jazzercise," I ask her, "only in water?"

"Are you kidding, Tone?"

"Tony, Tony, Tony," Dave scolds.

THE LORD OF WATSU

I FLOP on a lounge chair in a terrace of succulents. Smoke from burning pine billows above the fire pit. I peer over an aloe. Evo's waist deep in the pool. She's got on her black bikini with the white skull-and-crossbones pattern. Dave slips his left arm under her buns, supporting her shoulders with his right. He whispers. Her eyes close. He takes her wrist, pulls her close, and holds her. I imagine Dave as a god who's fallen for a mortal. He caresses her right ankle and lifts her leg. She arches her foot. He spins her tenderly in the water, her body circling his. He repeats this with her left and floats her over to the falls. They embrace beside the cascading water. I don't blame Dave for admiring my woman. Evo's hazel eyes and upturned nose conjure up images of castles and princesses. She was a Vegas showgirl out of high school and became an aerial artist. Her long legs flew over the drunks at the Ghost Bar. Carl, the bar manager, became her boyfriend. Carl's gambling debts at Bellagio got them in trouble, but she remained loyal even after he developed a heroin problem. A card shark threatened to take them on a one-way ride into the desert. Carl vanished on All Saints' Day. The shark wanted Evo to repay Carl's debts, so she got on a Greyhound bound for San Diego.

The sun drops behind Sheep Mountain. The pool turns purple.

"Fiber optics," Dave calls out to me. All colors east of yellow flash: lavender, green, and turquoise. He hugs Evo as the water goes violet. He climbs out and lights poolside torches. Evo eases up the granite incline, her arms and legs covered with violet water beads. She lights the final torch. Dave hugs her again. They're the couple you see in ads for once-in-a-lifetime getaways to romantic destinations.

Cosmo sticks his wet nose in my face.

I pat him ferociously.

*   *   *

Evo and I wake each morning to a creature symphony of door-pecking hens, howling roosters, and grumbling goats. A hen and her chick got in yesterday. Sudzy charged the chick and the hen nipped Sudzy. Now the princess has a new respect for fowl. We've been bums for two weeks. Dave does all the cooking, including serving us breakfast in bed. The sun breaks late over the mountain and the dome stays cool. Dave said outlaws hid at Nirvana in the days of stagecoaches, tin star sheriffs, and posses. At times I feel like an outlaw, as if men on horseback are galloping through tumbleweeds tracking me down. The only sign of life so far was a hot-air balloon floating like a renegade cloud over the mesas.

Strange dreams haunt me. In one, the dome's on fire and I'm beating at flames with wet burlap. In another, Evo marries Kurt Cobain at Caesar's Palace. Last night, she waltzed with Dave around a pool that kept expanding until it swallowed the desert. Maybe my dreams are linked to the 'shrooms. Dave dipped them in crème de menthe to kill their bitterness and took us on an adventure. We hiked through Serpent Flats, a level stretch across the highway swarming with lizards, horned toads, and snakes. Evo loved their eyes and iridescent scales. We followed snake trails through pink sand and it was only the tambourine-like jingling from rattlers that turned us back.

Dave says we can leave anytime. I know he wants us to have our freedom, but wishes we'd stay. He needs help with minor repairs, turbine maintenance, and simple things like harvesting and caring for the animals. Yesterday I dug out my rod and fished the pond. I fried sunfish for dinner and Evo made fruit salad. I just used my nail gun to replace five splintering shingles on the dome's roof and now I'm in the goat pen with Dave and Evo. The Nubians crowd Evo, and she looks worried clutching a basket of carrots. A nanny nudges Evo's bare leg with her nose and a kid licks her knee. Another kid nips at her leopard sneakers. Evo pulls a carrot and holds it out. A billy butts the nanny aside, and Evo raises the carrot. The billy stands on his haunches trying to reach it. "Does he bite?" she asks.

Dave chuckles. "Big Boy only nibbles."

I snatch a carrot and two kids charge over. Their tails flick as they take turns gnawing it.

"When you guys leave," Dave tells us, "head for water. Steer clear of the ocean. Find fresh water, like a lake, river, or stream. Desert dwellers will perish when the wells run dry."

Evo scrunches her nose. "Will they run dry?"

"Eventually."

"I'd consider Mexico," I say.

Big Boy rubs against Dave's leg like a cat. "Forget Mexico, Tony. The drug kings took over after Avenida Revolución got torched. They own Baja and hunt gringos for sport. Follow the 101 north to Oregon."

Evo gives the first nanny a carrot. "Who told you this, Daver?"

"BHRO."

"What's that?" I ask.

"The Brotherhood of Ham Radio Operators. These guys are the last gasp of freedom and pioneer spirit on the airwaves. Most operate off the grid, on solar power like me. My ham tower's on Turbine Hill and I've got pals as high as Vancouver."

"Oregon's safe?" I ask.

"It depends. Eugene and the coastal towns are battle zones. The residents of Ashland are slaves to a cult. Redmond's brother-versus-brother. High radiation levels in Portland. Go to Crater Lake. It's smaller than Tahoe but deeper and not tainted with poison. Plenty of clean water. Wizard Island's off the western shore so if you camped there it would be like living in a lava castle surrounded by the biggest moat in the world."

"How far is Crater Lake?" Evo asks.

"700 miles, as the crow flies. That pool on Wizard Island stays warm until Autumn Equinox."

"Pool?" I go.

"Emerald Pool. Cut by nature right out of the rock, fifty meters wide."

"Come with us," I tell Dave.

"And leave Nirvana? Not on your life."

Dave wants to give us something, so we finish up feeding the goats and leave the pen. We follow him through the eucalyptus behind the dome into the garage. He pulls gear and boxes off the shelves and puts everything on a butcher block workbench: a pocket water micro-filter, stainless steel water bottles, U.S. Army MREs, Scout FireSteel to start fires, a medical kit with everything from sutures to potassium iodide tablets, waterproof parkas, solar flashlights, night vision goggles, rolls of Duck Tape, a portable solar shower, and QuikClot clotting sponges.

"You can't use this stuff?" I ask him.

"I'm off the grid and self-sufficient. Besides, the Dynamic Duo might need it on Wizard Island." Dave slides open a cabinet drawer and pulls out a sword. The blade's not long and it has a silvery sheath. "Catch," he goes, tossing it.

I catch the copper hilt. The sword has strips of overlapping leather for a handle and feels heavy for its size.

"Check out the blade, Tony."

I snap off the sheath and hold up a wide, double-edged blade that shines like silver bullion. I do a half-swing. It feels well-balanced and solid.

Evo backs up. "What kinda sword is it?"

"Not a sword at all, Vegas. That's a Tuareg dagger, used by the nomads in North Africa. It's got a nickel sheath and a multi-layered blade as fine as a samurai sword."

I swing again. The Tuareg's a dagger on steroids, one long enough to be considered a sword yet possessing two-sided killing power.

Dave stacks boxes of MREs. "That Tuareg could save your life someday, Tony."

Evo fingers a clotting sponge. "Hope it doesn't come to that."

*   *   *

Evo and I sit on the casita's deck in oak chairs. The sundowners carry the scent of pine down from Sheep Mountain. Evo's got on her white halter-top and aqua shorts. Her hair's streaked blonde from the sun and her shoulders are dark. I gaze into the Mojave as the land turns a dusky red. The first frog sounds like a French horn. The second's a bassoon. A cricket chimes in.

Dave shuffles out of the casita in moccasins. He's balancing a spacedrum on his shoulder. "I put on Yangjin Lamu," he says, sitting beside Evo.

A female voice cuts out of the casita and over the deck. Her song is shrill and unsettling but she settles down into a humming melody. Dave taps notes out of the spacedrum. I turn inward. I'm troubled by thoughts of nuclear fallout, a future of masters and slaves, and a wasteland not meant for babies. Knowing I'm with Evo keeps me steady. My love for her is the beacon that guides me out of dark places.

Lamu finishes her song, and Dave lowers his spacedrum. "Time for din-din," he goes.

"Can I help?" Evo asks.

"Certainly, Vegas."

Dave takes her hand and they head inside. The desert turns to shadow. A bird cries from the timber bamboo. A tuba-like croak joins an orchestra of French horns and bassoons. The crickets sound like violins. The sky turns mauve and the big stars burn through.

Dave returns with cast iron pots of vegan curry and white rice. Evo carries condiments in coconut cups: shredded coconut, mango chutney, and slivered dates. They place everything on an oak table with tweed runners. I set the table with stoneware plates and sterling spoons. Dave gives me an ice cream scooper and I scoop balls of rice from a pot onto the plates. Evo lights the deck torches. We put Dave in the middle and sit facing the Mojave. We join hands and Dave blesses the desert. He asks God to forgive him for any harm he's caused in the past and to free him of bad feelings for Justin. He prays for our safety if we decide to leave. "Enough talk," Dave goes, "let's eat."

We take turns ladling curry over the rice and spooning on condiments.

Cosmo sits down on the deck, raises a paw, and whines.

Dave tosses a rice ball and Cosmo catches it in his mouth.

Evo samples the curry. "Wowie," she goes, "this is another masterpiece."

I sample the curry. It's spicy-hot and the sauce is thick. A comet flies over Nirvana toward the mesas. "Quick, Dave," I go, "make a wish."

"I wish for a life partner," he says, plucking a bottle of Powder Keg out of a silver caddy.

"Are we celebrating something?" Evo asks.

He fills three glasses with the syrah. "Today's my thirty-eighth birthday."

She leans over and kisses him. "Happy birthday, Daver."

I raise my glass. "To a gentleman and a scholar."

We drink.

Dave seems bummed during dinner. He refuses more syrah and picks at his food. He stares into the night as if searching for a distant fire. The Frog Concerto rages, but he seems oblivious to it. I tell stories about the great nights we shared in Oceanside.

"My days of bourbon gloom," Dave sighs. He confesses that, if it weren't for Nirvana, he'd have ended it years ago.

"Don't think like that," Evo scolds. "Promise?"

"A palmist said I wouldn't see forty, Vegas."

"Hogwash," I say.

"Hear that eerie silence, Tony?" he asks.

"I only hear frogs."

"I hear it in the Mojave. That silence makes me feel that I'm already dead, but that my spirit hasn't left my body yet."

"Are those the 'shrooms talking?" I kid.

I wish I could find someone for Dave, but Pinyon Crest isn't exactly crawling with single men. This new world makes you feel distrustful and lonesome, especially when nobody's around to care about you. You've got to grab happiness where you can find it and hold on tight.

THEY CAME

A RUMBLE of *bup-bup-bups* jolts me from my Powder Keg stupor. The noise rattles the shingled roof. I pretend it's a summer storm or a turbine failing. I reach for Evo—she's not there. I sit up. Horizontal bars of light spill through the blinds. A hand pries open two slats.

"Babe?" I call.

"Outsiders," Evo says.

I pull up my boxers. "Where's the princess?"

"Under your nightstand."

I join her at the window. Motorcycles circle the hen house, their exhaust pipes blowing demonic blasts. The casita's porch light comes on. Three bikers pull up beside the goat pen and kill their engines. They've got black helmets. Their black leathers gleam like oil. Chickens flee the hen house with broods of chicks. One hen flaps her wings trying to fly. I hear no pleading from the Nubians, and the frogs in the pond go mute.

Dave walks out to his porch in his white bathrobe and shuts the door behind him. Cosmo barks inside the casita.

"Good evening," Dave begins. Nirvana is stone cold quiet and he's only fifty yards away.

A biker clears his throat. "Hate troublin' you like this, amigo."

"No trouble at all," Dave replies.

Evo nudges me. "What should we do?"

"No lights," I whisper. "Stay clear of windows and keep the blinds shut." I drop and scramble on my hands and knees. Evo's right behind me as I slide the Panther out from under the bed. I sneak into the bathroom, crank open the tiny window, and shove out the screen. I rest the stock on the ledge and sight through the scope. The bikers squat on the wide seats of their hogs. The fat one teases the goats with a "Pop goes the Weasel" rhyme. The guy near the trough peels off his helmet. He's got a black beard and a checkered do-rag. I stick his nose in the crosshairs. He dangles his helmet off the handlebar and swaggers over to the casita. "Gotta collect on a debt from a squaw down the road," he tells Dave. "Saw your gate and didn't think you'd mind a heido-ho. You know Cody Tabeshaw?"

Dave strokes his goatee. "No. Can't say that I do."

"Never heard his name?"

"It doesn't sound familiar."

"Sure 'bout that?"

"I'd remember a name like Cody."

The biker coughs up phlegm and spits. "Mighty peculiar Cody livin' so close and you never crossin' paths."

"Wait," Dave blurts, "is he a thin man with a big turquoise buckle?"

"Sure is. When you see 'im last?"

"Easter Sunday. He said he was leaving for good.'"

"Say where he was headin'?"

"East. Omaha, I think."

"Omaha? Now why would that sonuvabitch go all the way to Omaha with kin in Indio?"

"I don't know why," Dave says, hunching his back. "You boys from Palm Desert?"

"Boys? Who you callin' 'boys?'"

"I didn't mean to insult you. I'm Dave Draco, from Oceanside."

"Fair enough. I'm Bart, and Royce's the one puffin' the cigar. Fat one's JP."

JP shifts his weight and nearly falls off his chopper. His Nazi helmet glimmers in the porch light, and it looks like it's welded to his skull. "Ain't so fat," he whimpers.

"JP's fatter'n a holiday pig," Royce snickers. He pulls off his helmet, hops off his bike, and puffs his way over to the goat pen.

The bathroom door creaks. I lower the Panther. Evo hands me the binoculars, along with my holstered Beretta. I strap on the holster and max-zoom the binos.

Bart stands at the edge of the porch and slaps a support post with an open hand. "Here by your lonesome, Dave?"

"Yes."

"Nobody else around?"

"Not a soul."

Bart points at the dome. "Who's in your hippie house?"

Shock waves race through me. My hands go numb. I hope Dave doesn't spill the beans. I zero in on my friend's face—his lips quiver and his eyes blink fast.

"Built that for guests," he replies, looking down. "But I haven't had a guest in years."

"No old lady?"

"Never been married. I guess I'm a misanthrope."

"Just you and the pooch?"

Dave hides his hands in the pockets of his robe. "Just me and Cosmo."

"Dog surely hates us," Royce grouses, flicking ashes into the trough. He's got broad shoulders and a Dough Boy gut. Deep sockets give him skull-like eyes. He heads for the casita and a rooster pecks his boot. He kicks it and the bird screeches off. He steps up on the porch and peers through a window. Cosmo snarls inside. "Well, Missy Thrope," Royce says, "us boys are mighty parched from our journey. Any beer to be had?"

"No beer here," Dave replies.

"Whiskey?"

"No hard liquor."

"How come?"

"I had a drinking problem."

"He's a fuckin' alky," JP squeals, "like brother Joe!"

"Any water?" Bart presses.

"I've got a pond," Dave answers.

"Well, aren't you the Rainbow Dick," Royce snarls, standing shoulder to shoulder with Bart. "You offer us piss when you flush with the pure stuff?"

"I have running water, if that's what you'd prefer."

"Prefer," he mocks. "This dude's an ass pirate."

"Dave," Bart goes, "is what Royce says true?"

"No."

"Bullshit," says Royce, flicking his stub at a loose hen. "He's the fuckin' Queen of Pinyon Crest. Hey, JP, he look queer?"

JP flaps his arms and nearly falls off his chopper again. "Chicken," he sings off-key, "chicken, chicken, chicken queen."

"Careful, JP," Bart warns, "Dave might be a chubby chaser."

"Look't his lips, bro," goes Royce. "Bet he can suck pearls outta an oyster."

I lower the binos and lift the Panther. I work the bolt action and a bullet leaps into the chamber. My crosshairs go back and forth between Bart and Royce. Sudzy jumps on the ledge and rubs her chin against the barrel.

"Je-sus," I stammer.

Evo plucks her off.

I sight again. Dave takes his hands out of his pockets. He looks weak standing there in moccasins and terrycloth. "Come back tomorrow," he goes. "I'll give you all the water you need."

Burt belches. "Where's Cody?"

"Gone, just like I told you."

"You wouldn't mind us havin' a look see, now would you? Not that we don't trust you or anythin'."

Dave crosses his arms. "Our visit's over."

I put Bart's neck in the crosshairs. I imagine steel ripping through his throat.

Bart smacks Dave. Dave hunches over, holding his cheek.

"This is how you treat three tired hombres?" Royce scolds Dave.

"I want you all to leave."

"Step aside," Bart orders.

Dave straightens his posture and says nothing.

Royce flicks his stub at him.

Bart reaches for something inside his jacket—a barrel gleams. A *boom-boom* tears through Nirvana and the impact sends Dave backwards. He falls against the front door and crumples.

My first bullet rips through Bart's neck. The second smashes into JP's helmet. Royce is sprinting past the trough when I fire the third. He reaches his bike and slams the kick-starter. The engine sputters. I crosshair his chest. Royce looks over at the dome and slams again as the fourth bullet flies. The Harley roars to life, he revs the throttle, and zooms off. His headlight burns through the orchard toward the highway.

Evo runs out of the dome wearing only a black bra and panties. I try keeping up. I hurdle a hen and stumble in my boxers. Evo reaches Dave first. He lies beside the door and blood snakes over the tiles. "Hel-lo," he mumbles.

I rip open his robe and see two wounds in his chest.

Evo runs back to the dome.

Dave's eyelids flutter.

"Stay with me, Dave. Don't you give up."

Evo returns with clotting sponges. We try to slow the bleeding by pressing them against the wounds.

Evo puts his head in her lap. "Oh, Daver."

"I have to go get that bastard," I tell her.

"You go nowhere."

"He'll bring more bikers," I say, standing. "We'll never get out alive."

She cradles Dave's head and weeps. "You fuckin' asshole, Tony."

I hustle back to the dome and pull on my cargo pants and high-tops. I make sure my Beretta's loaded and tighten the straps of the shoulder holster. I fire up Rovy in the garage and rip past the goat pen into the orchard. Moths bounce off my headlights. I crank a sharp left at the Joshua tree and burn rubber flooring it on the highway. I'm sure Royce is heading back to the desert cities. I've got to catch him before the hairpins. I hit 100. The highway drops into the desert's bowels and I'm redlining it. Where the fuck is he? I make a fist and punch the dash. I spot a red dot, one the size of Mars. The dot disappears around a curve but reappears when the highway straightens. I close in. That must be Royce. I keep the pedal pinned until the dot becomes a taillight. It's moving slowly, maybe 80. I creep closer. The rider has no helmet. I ram him with my bumper and the Harley weaves. I ram again—the bike careens and launches off the highway.

I shift to 4WD and give chase through boulders and scrub. He slips through a web of pinions. He's easy to spot with his headlight blazing. I'm forced into a gulley that sends Rovy's front end slamming into the ground. I mow down cacti and catch him skirting a wash. I crank a wicked right and sideswipe Royce. The bike flies— it hits an outcropping and Royce lands spread-eagle in a giant agave. I blind him with my brights and pull the Beretta. I walk toward his execution as desert rock crunches under my high-tops.

Royce studies his hand. "So," he goes, "you're the sniper."

I pull back on the hammer until it locks.

He bites out a thorn and spits. "Dave's girlfriend, right?"

"I have a wife, you bastard."

"Let's settle this mano-a-mano. Whatcha say?"

"The way you settled Dave?"

Royce eases out of the agave and dusts off his vest. "Wanna show you something."

I follow him to the Harley. He grabs the handlebar and leans it against a ponderosa. The headlight's shattered. The tank's dented and leaking. He pulls a chain and a guthook knife from his saddlebag. "Go ahead," Royce says, "shoot me. But that won't satisfy you, not in the long run."

"Say what?"

"You and me, we're fuckin' gladiators. We die with honor. Use an ax, blade, or tire iron. Whatever feels bitchin'. I'm waiting to die in the Roman Coliseum." He sinks the knife's blade into the tree.

I lower my gun. He's right. I do want blood. Honest blood, not blood spilled by cowardly execution. I return to Rovy and fling open the cargo door. I spot the fubar. I snatch it and it seems like just what the doctor ordered. But it feels too heavy. The Kukri machete is wedged between my tackle box and a water jug. I grab the koa handle and yank off the burlap sheath. I swing and air *whooshes* past the blade. I spy through my window—Royce waits beside his bike.

I notice the road flares in my cargo door panel. I grab one, pop the cap, and strike the rough edge against the flare's tip. A pink flame sparks to life, casting a pink halo over the desert. I step into the open, with the Kukri in my left and the flare in my right. "Just us two in the Roman Coliseum," I tell Royce.

"Fuck," he goes, pulling his knife out of the tree.

He swings the chain. We close ground. He twirls faster and faster and works in more and more links to lengthen the loops. I duck and the chain whizzes over my head. I swing the Kukri at the next pass but miss. I try again—metal strikes metal. I can't get close enough to stab with the blade or burn with the flare. The chain comes again and whacks my temple. The next loop smashes my jaw with such force that I drop the machete and fall to my knees. Blood oozes through my teeth. "Die," Royce goes, thrusting the guthook. I dodge the blade and jam the flare in his face. His flesh gives, as if I'm pushing into clay. His head jerks and the fire goes with him.

Royce yanks out the flare and embers spark above him. "My

fuckin' eye!" he hollers and hurls the flare into the desert.

It smells like bad barbecue. The Kukri's blade glints in Rovy's lights. I roll over and snatch the handle. Royce slashes with the guthook. I swing the Kukri up—a diagonal line from his right cheek to his left eye zips open and blood pours out.

"No!" he moans.

I get up wielding the Kukri.

He wobbles to his Harley and swings a leg over the wide seat. "If I don't kill you," he snarls, "Joe will. Never forget, Joe's a-comin'."

"Who the fuck's Joe?"

He kicks the chopper to life. Blood spills into his one good eye and he wipes it away. He cranks the throttle, and the headlight flickers. I hold the Kukri over my shoulder like a ball bat. Part of me wants to die. But a bigger part wants to kill. "Wa-hoo!" I yelp, my cry booming across the Mohave to warm the cold hearts of snakes. Royce lurches forward and he's upon me. I grip the koa handle with both hands and step into my swing. The blade catches Royce flush on the neck and peels off his head. The bike continues on with his headless torso and crashes into a saguaro.

*　　　*　　　*

I luck out finding a trail and 4WD it through a dark gulley. I drive with the window open and the churning tires calm me. I always knew there was a monster inside me. Chuckers the Clown tripped me in sixth grade and punched me bloody until I grabbed his throat and squeezed so hard he got toad eyes. I can't control the monster. It's like trying to stop a truck without brakes rolling down a hill. I was certain the monster would land me in jail, but I wanted to be behind bars so it could feed on fellow prisoners. I must be nuts.

*   *   *

I find a nanny goat wandering the highway near the Joshua tree. I get out and put her in cargo. I drive through Nirvana hoping this whole thing's been a nightmare and that I'm really asleep back at the dome. I park beside the casita and turn the goat loose. JP and Bart lie where I shot them. Hens peck their bodies. A bedspread covers a body on the porch. The Frog Concerto plays as if nothing happened.

Evo runs off the porch over to my window. "Did you?" she asks.

I nod. "Is Dave?"

"Yes. I tried everything, Tony. You've gotta believe me."

"Is Cosmo okay?"

"He's safe inside with me and Sudzy."

"I need a drink."

"I need one too."

ALOHA, PINYON CREST

ASHES RAIN on Nirvana. The stench from Palm Springs taints the dome and drives us out at dawn. The air's so bad it leaves gray powder under my nose and around my nostrils. Evo found a surgical mask and put it on. The roosters won't crow. The chickens gather on the casita porch and the goats don't drink from the trough. Cosmo's camped in the ice plant. The wind rattles the eucalyptus so violently the branches sound as if they're made of bone. Turbine Hill's *womp-ah-womp-ah-womp* sounds like a beating heart. Evo hunts through the casita trying to find an address for Dave's folks. I located the ham radio but only got the garbled voice of a trucker in Vancouver. Nirvana seems foreign. It feels as though a stranger owns it now and we're no longer welcome.

I walk the vegan rows, remembering Dave frying omelets while Evo gathered strawberries. Our last meal with Dave was dinner last night and I can still hear him playing the spacedrum. Cosmo whines from the ice plant.

I stomp my high-tops. "Here, boy."

Cosmo keeps his head down.

Evo hurries over the porch with a shovel. She looks like a nurse wearing that mask. I wave. She gives a half-hearted wave back.

I've got mixed emotions about splitting. I've bonded with the animals and even the frogs. I love the high desert with the mesas, arroyos, pines, and big sky. I picture the irrigation failing, berries shriveling, and rows getting choked by weeds. I see the goats wandering off to Sheep Mountain. I want to protect them, but there are no guarantees bikers won't show up, especially after I found a tracking bug on Burt's chopper. Evo and I stand a better chance on the run. Guarding Nirvana would be futile because danger can come from any direction at any time. I searched Bart and JP and found crystal meth, gold coins, silver rounds, chewing tobacco, and an IOU signed by Tabeshaw. Evo helped me roll their bodies up a plywood ramp into the bed of Dave's old Ford. I drove five miles into the desert and pushed them off like logs into Vulture Gulch.

*   *   *

I wheelbarrow Dave to the timber bamboo and start digging beside the highest spike. Cosmo watches from the granite lip of the pool. Evo takes off her mask and takes a turn when I tire. The ground gets hard a foot down so I use a metal bar with a sharp blade to cut through. I do the cutting while Evo shovels. In four hours we have a hole three feet deep and we bury Dave. Evo helps me shimmy over a large tiki to mark his grave. We hold hands and stand in silence. Cosmo sniffs the tiki and hunkers down on the dirt.

"Forgot my prayers," I tell Evo.

The wind rustles the bamboo. Leaves cascade into the pool.

"Dear God," Evo says, "bless our friend Dave. Welcome this prince among men into your Kingdom."

*   *   *

I open the goat pen. We wave carrots outside the gate but the Nubians refuse to leave. Finally a billy ventures out and nibbles Evo's offering. The nannies follow. The kids join their mothers. They munch all the carrots and wander over to the garden.

"Will they survive, Tony?" Evo asks.

"Sure," I answer. "Lotsa water in the pond and the garden's peaking. If irrigation fails, they'll still have plenty of weeds and scrub."

"And ice plant?"

"A Nubian delicacy."

"What about the chickens and roosters?"

"Tough as nails," I tell her. "They'll have bugs and snails for decades and can pig out when the corn ripens."

"Sure?"

"Dave chose the right animals, Babe. And the Frog Concerto will go on."

*   *   *

I pull cactus pulp and pieces of tumbleweed out of Rovy's grill. I load in bags of fruit and avos into cargo. I find gas in a secret shed and lash six steel cans to the roof rack with bungee cords. I roll the Harleys into the shed.

Cosmo's lapping water from the trough.

"Wanna go, boy?" I coax.

He trots over to the open cargo door, stands on his haunches, and rests his paws on the bumper.

"In, boy."

He tilts his head and gives me a curious look.

"You'll have fun in Oregon," I promise.

Cosmo leaps in and curls up on a bed of sleeping bags and blankets.

The goats are dining on strawberries. Evo hugs a nanny and heads over to Rovy. She's wearing a chartreuse halter and matching spandex shorts. "Crater Lake?" she asks.

"Dave wanted us too."

She slips the strap off her shoulder and hands me the canteen.

I unscrew the cap and swallow. The icy water tastes like metal.

*   *   *

We leave Nirvana at noon. The shadow off Sheep Mountain makes it seem like dusk. I hang a left at the Joshua tree. Evo spots a hawk gliding over the mesas. Cosmo's sleeping in cargo. Sudzy's on

Evo's lap. The princess has been cool so far with our new passenger. The mountain's shadow stretches miles down the highway. A bright yellow desert and a blinding sky await.

*   *   *

We glide the Palms to Pines Highway. Evo blasts the AC. Pines give way to cacti and bitterbrush. I feel like a balloon buffeted by a cruel wind. When you reconnect with a long lost amigo if feels as if the years apart were only days, but losing that friend after reuniting makes you feel old.

I gaze into the Mojave. The mesas look like a backdrop for a school play. I pass the spot before the hairpins where I forced Royce off the road. Something breaks out of the heat waves ahead. I see silver flashes where metal catches the sun. It's wide and low, like a flatbed pulling a trailer. I realize what I'm seeing is not one thing but something made of many parts with dozens of drivers. It's a swarm of motorcycles and half the swarm is on our side.

"Jesus," I say.

Evo sinks Sudzy in the carrier. "Do we fight, Tony?"

"No way. Better duck down."

"Why?"

"They'll want you."

Evo slips the carrier on the floor mat and crouches beside it.

The swarm flies in v-formation. A fat guy's out front. Most

wear black leather vests and do-rags. I ease up on the pedal. The fat guy raises his hand as we close. The bikers in our lane veer to the other side. The fat guy salutes me and the swarm roars by. I keep an eye on the rear-view mirror until they disappear.

"Aloha 'oe," I say.

"Where'd you put the tracker?" Evo asks.

"Vulture Gulch, in Burt's pocket."

"Was that wise, Tony?"

"We'll be a hundred miles away by the time they find him."

* * *

The desert cities are one big war zone of smoke, looting, and gunfire. Locals cross Palm Springs Boulevard like zombies, a dead look in their eyes. A corgi runs the gutter dragging its leash. Boys scavenge piles of garbage. An old man loads a revolver under a hotel canopy while two women look on. A primered-gray truck with a machine gun mounted on its bed circles the Convention Center.

Cosmo crawls forward and sticks his head between the front seats.

"Bet he's hungry," Evo says.

I pull over. Couples jog in a field of buffalo grass. I open the backseat door for Cosmo. The wind blows like a hair dryer. I'm glad Rovy has a new water pump and fresh antifreeze.

Evo puts two bowls on the sidewalk and pours kibble in one. Cosmo eats while she spills canteen water into the second.

"Didn't he eat at Nirvana?" I ask.

"Only Sudzy. You need to pill her."

I find the princess curled up on Evo's seat. She looks so small. I want to attack the cancer and break its deadly DNA strands, end its ability to replicate. The pills are my weapons but the enemy continues to advance. I see pain in her body. Am I making her suffer needlessly? No. Sudzy still purrs. She still eats and grooms. She wants to live.

*   *   *

I reach the 10 and hightail it west. There are no mesas here, only the distant San Gabriels that look blue through the wisps of smoke and ash. It seems like the Mojave will never end and that we're destined to be in it until the first nuclear blast. Crater Lake is pure fantasy, a blue eye of promise in a dream. I feel like a wimp who can't find safe haven and is only as good as his next gallon of gas. No fuel means we're finito. I always thought I'd end up in a small town with a cool wife, trusted neighbors, and super kids. I'm homeless. The future terrifies me, but I'll never tell Evo. She needs me to make the hard decisions.

"Carrot?" Evo asks me.

"I hate carrots."

"You hate all vegetables."

"I love rhubarb."

"You say that only 'cause I can't get any." She opens a plastic bag and pulls out a strawberry.

I open my mouth and she sticks it in. I bite down and see Dave walking the rows. I remember Evo's fruit salads served on a deck overlooking an expanse so great it made me feel safe. Part of me wants to do a 180 and return to Nirvana. But what about Joe? Maybe the casita and dome are burning. Maybe he's roasting goats and shooting chickens after finding Burt. The more miles I put between Pinyon Crest and us the better. I pluck Super Shorty out of my door compartment and pass it to Evo.

"What's this for?" she asks.

"Keep it on your side," I tell her, "you're a natural."

*   *   *

I pull up to the pumps in Owl. The Texaco sign's shattered. We get out and stretch. Evo crosses her legs and does the Eagle pose. No sign of Ray. I stick a nozzle in my tank but no gas comes out. A ratchet and sockets balance on the curved hood of a garbage can between pumps. A truck outside the garage has its hood up. Ray's jumpsuit lies crumpled in the dirt.

"There," Evo goes, pointing north.

A root beer-colored llama with a white forehead plods toward the mountains. "Refugee," I tell her, "from the petting zoo."

"Poor darling needs water."

"No way. Llamas are like camels."

"Quit being stingy."

When Evo gets like this I always give in. She believes good deeds invite good karma, especially when helping animals. I find a plastic bucket in the garage and we drive out to the llama. I crack the cargo door. Cosmo nudges his way out and circles the llama like a sheep-herding dog. I tip water from a jug into the bucket. The llama blinks as the water sloshes back and forth.

Evo sticks in her hand and splashes. "Come on, Sahara," she goes.

"You've already named him?" I ask.

"Her."

"No balls?"

"Right."

Sahara sniffs the bucket and chews the plastic rim. Evo splashes again. Sahara dips in her long tongue and the water's gone in seconds. I refill the bucket and she sucks that up too.

"Give Sahara more," Evo tells me.

"We need this water."

"Give her my ration."

I fill the bucket a third time. Sahara guzzles every drop. Her brown eyes look sad, as if she's resigned to never finding a mate in the new world. Evo offers a carrot and Sahara devours it. Next comes an orange followed by strawberries. Cosmo barks. Sahara swings a back leg and a hoof narrowly misses Cosmo.

"Time to boogie," I say.

Evo rubs Sahara's forehead. "Goodbye, sweet girl."

SATAN'S BARB

THE 215 LEADS us to massive pile-ups and gangs of looters tearing through trunks and cargo. I weave between lanes to avoid car seats, jacks, luggage, an crates of bottled water. Our GPS is busted. Or maybe the satellite feeding it got blown to astral dust. The GPS lady thinks we're somewhere in Utah. Evo starts unfolding our maps. We need a northern corridor through the Sierras, one that's a straight shot for the coast. Evo says our only chance is the 10 west. We go off-road at West Covina to avoid a barricade. The foothills are crawling with punks on ATVs and armed teens. We return to the 10. The emergency lane clears. Monterery Park seems untouched, except for a chorus of sirens and the stench of tear gas. Tanks idle at Pioneer Park in El Monte.

Evo examines a map. "Get ready," she warns.

I look west. Skyscrapers loom before us. I want to avoid inner cities but LA seems unavoidable. "City of Angels?" I ask.

"Only way, Tone."

The emergency lane stays open. I crush two bicycles in our path. Suburban pockets give way to an industrial fringe of refineries, monstrous oil storage reservoirs, and warehouses. An electrical stench mixes with the stink of diesel. A splinter of gas blue sky is lodged in the horizon. We enter LA's web of overpasses. The Planetarium smolders. The clock tower of the County Courthouse is frozen at twelve and no traffic moves on the streets below. City Hall leans like the Tower of Pisa. Smoke shrouds the Hollywood billboards. I swerve around a stalled rig. The *boom-ah-boom* of heavy artillery makes pedestrians on Wilshire Boulevard scramble. The Hollywood Bowl has become a staging area—cargo trucks, troop carriers, and Hummers surround the Bowl. A black helicopter lands on the stage. Soldiers in black uniforms spy from the NBC Building's rooftop. I remember a rumor about an apocalypse bunker under the Coliseum. Something wet on my neck makes me to flinch—it's Cosmo's nose.

"Good boy," I say, reaching back to pat him.

The smoke lifts. The gas blue sky expands on the city's western edge. We reach Santa Monica and head north on Highway 1, passing fields strewn with white crosses and roadside graves festooned with marigolds. Cowboys trot horses on the sidewalk. Bicyclists glide over pedestrian walkways. A cop in shorts directs traffic around a helicopter that crashed on the boardwalk.

I continue north to Malibu and crack my window. The breeze feels good. Umbrellas dot the sand but the beach is mostly deserted. Sails skim the Pacific. A waterspout churns beyond the sails. The ocean disappears when we hit a stretch of beachfront mansions. Collections of heavy furniture sit on the sidewalk, everything from grandfather clocks to leather couch islands to tiki bars. It resembles a

Going Out of Business sale. Wrinkled men sit on beach chairs drinking beer.

*   *   *

The sign says we've entered SATAN'S BARB. The former Santa Barbara has become a checkerboard of black plateaus and barren hills. It stinks of wildfire. The Pacific looks gray through burnt coastal pines. I check my gauges: the temperature's normal but the Check Engine light glows. We're below a quarter tank. I take the ramp for downtown. A boy with a Mohawk stands at the intersection of Hope Avenue and State Street. Two men are stoning something in the coyote brush.

I pull over. "Why the stoning?" I ask Mohawk Boy.

"Rattler bit their pit bull."

"Any gas?"

"Depends."

Evo passes him a bag of fruit.

Mohawk Boy bites into a strawberry. "Ajax is your man."

"Where's he at?"

"PCH and La Cumbre."

"Thanks," I tell him.

We tool down Hope Avenue to an iron gate with CALVARY CEMETERY in Goth letters. I catch a whiff of raw sewage. A urinal's wedged in the crotch of an oak tree behind the gate. A man runs between headstones. "Halp," he goes, "she's killin' me!" He hurls himself on the gate and pulls himself up. A naked woman grabs his ankles and hangs on until he falls.

"Fun times," I tell Evo.

We pass orange groves and I go right when we reach PCH. A park has a great view of the Pacific. The water isn't gray anymore and green tubes roll in off the open ocean. Surfers shred the waves and girls play on an inflatable mattress in the shallows. Santa Cruz Island floats like a lazy whale on the horizon. Everything seems safe. But Dave told me the Phoenix Army marched here after taking LA. The Santa Barbara geezers torched their mansions and fled to Santa Cruz Island on catamarans. They'd paid mercenaries to fortify their new island sanctuary and the mercenaries earned their denaro firing rockets at the PA's assault boats. But islands can be taken, even with great guard dogs. The Fed thought Catalina was impenetrable so the VP took over Avalon. The PA parachuted warriors in. The VP fled by hydrofoil, but pirates capsized him. They held the VP hostage at Nixon's old San Clemente beach house and ransomed him for a billion in gold.

We skirt the burnt-out shells of mansions. Evo spots La Cumbre Road and we cut through a peach-colored subdivision that reminds me of Portico. The asphalt turns to dirt. The dirt road leads to a warehouse surrounded by a cyclone fence. I find a hole in the fence and follow the tracks through a field of flowering weeds. The warehouse is tagged and there's a cartoon sketch of a blond monster lifting a wimp out of a chair by the neck. AJAX'S BAR is painted in red on the steel entry door. I creep past a dirt lot filled with choppers, ATVs, and muscle cars. I pull over beside an old-fashioned gas pump in back of the warehouse.

"No way," Evo grumbles.

"We need gas, Babe."

"How low are we?"

"Below a quarter tank."

"Last time we take chances," she goes.

I get out and Evo follows. Cosmo whimpers in cargo. I drop an arm over Evo's shoulder and we hot walk it past the lot. A hippie sits on an ATV smoking a joint. I hear the clang of metal striking metal—men in black leathers are fencing with foils. One's bleeding from the shoulder. The bleeding man swings wildly but misses. "Slow down, killer," the other man says.

We reach the steel door to Ajax's Bar. A mermaid's mounted above it—she's blonde with bright pink nipples and has skin down to her belly button. Her hips and butt sparkle with green scales.

A behemoth slouches in a barbershop chair beside the shut door. A bayonet's wedged between his thigh and the side of the chair. He's got needles stuck in his forehead. An Asian man with pigtail knots taps a needle into the behemoth's cheek and blood shoots out.

"Holy Christ!" wails the behemoth.

"What's wrong?" asks Evo.

"Bell's palsy," the Asian man answers.

The behemoth eyeballs me. "Patron or amigo?"

"Both," I answer.

"Say the magic word."

"Abracadabra."

"That's the old shit. Pretend you're Ali Baba, raghead of the desert."

"Open Sesame," I say but the door doesn't budge.

The behemoth takes another needle, this one to his temple. "Louder."

"Open Sesame!"

The door cranks open, as if hidden pulleys or hydraulics are moving it. I grab Evo's hand and we slip through. The door shuts behind us. It's dark. The only light comes from a row of flickering candles. It smells of cut cocaine, hard liquor, and leather. Red light spills through the slats of a saloon-type door. I swing the door open and follow Evo in. Chopper frames, tear-shaped tanks, and chrome manifolds hang on the walls. Leathers hang too, including tons of chick stuff: leather minis, cowhide bras, palomino panties, and buckskin garters. The warehouse floor is wall-to-wall black Berber carpet. Fans *wha-woomp* overhead. A jukebox plays, "Paint it Black." Girls in costume gyrate on the bar's chrome counter. An AJAX'S BAR sign spills red neon on the girls. A blonde Nurse pole dances using a steel support post. A French Maid in garters teases the toughs seated on stools around the bar. A School Girl wearing a paisley skirt skips a jump rope. A muscled bartender with spiked blond hair fills glasses, pops beer caps, and exchanges packets of white powder for bullion. Bouncers armed with shotguns stand on either side of the counter. A third bouncer is behind the bar. "Paint it Black" ends and the girls quit dancing. The men talk dirty to them. The girls sass them back. A biker with a Hell's Angels vest rips open a packet and spills powder over the counter. The French Maid drops and snorts it up with a straw.

I grab Evo's hand and tug her past the jukebox. All the bar stools are taken so we stand behind a seated buzz top who's snorting what smells like ether out of a vapor canister.

"Who's Ajax?" I ask the buzz top.

He keeps snorting.

Evo squeezes my hand. The French Maid unhooks a garter and the Hell's Angel flicks out his tongue. The Nurse unbuttons her dress, revealing a lacy white bra. The School Girl licks a rainbow lollipop.

"Time to boogie, Tony," Evo goes.

I cup my hands around my mouth. "Hey, fuckheads!" I say. "Where's that motherfucker Ajax?"

The dirty talk and flirting ends. All I hear are the churning fans and the clinking glasses.

The buzz top spins on his stool. His arms and shoulders are

tattooed with zombies and skulls. "Who you callin' motherfucker," he goes, "you fuckin' douche bag."

The bartender unlatches a half-door in the counter and has to go sideways to get through. He's as big as the cartoon monster on the warehouse wall and I feel like the wimp the monster's strangling. He's got a chin beard and bulky chrome earrings glimmer in his lobes. He crosses his arms when we're face to face. "I'm Ajax," he tells me, "whatcha want?"

"Gas," I tell him.

His eyes bulge. "Not a chance."

"We can trade."

"Tradin's for old maids, lightweight. I own everythin', includin' the Rover you pulled up in, the shirt on your back, even your old lady. Ain't that right, muchachos?"

A roar goes up, followed by catcalls and the *slap-slapping* of high fives.

"Can your lady dance?" he asks me.

"No."

"She'd better learn quick like, if you plan on seein' tomorrow."

Two bouncers frame Ajax in muscle and shotguns.

The holster presses against my ribs. I'm tempted to reach but there's no way to get off a shot before the shotguns belch.

"I'll do it," Evo tells Ajax. "I'll dance for premium."

"Don't do it, Evo," I mutter.

Ajax's eyes quit bulging. "Evo," he says, "I like that name. You any good, girl?"

"Numero uno at the Ghost Bar."

"Vamanos bitches!" Ajax says, waving at his girls.

The Nurse twirls the pole once more before descending a staircase down to the bar. The School Girl and the French Maid follow. Evo slips through the half-door and climbs the stairs. She's on the counter looking like a goddess in destroyed cut-offs, white halter, and leopard sneakers. The Hell's Angel whistles. Evo bows to a chorus of hollers. A woman wearing a fedora, the only woman at the bar, lights up a skinny cigar. Ajax tells his bouncers to beat it and extends a hand. We shake. "What's your name, lightweight?"

"Tony."

"Where y' headin'?"

"Oregon."

We watch Evo pace the counter. She drops and does a headstand on the chrome, her long legs bathed in red neon.

"What song, Evo?" Ajax shouts.

"Twenty-first century," Evo answers. "Got rope?"

"How 'bout chain?"

"Sure. Loop it over that crossbeam below the roof."

"Lucky," Ajax calls, "help this sweetheart out."

Lucky, a tiny man in a green vest, joins Evo on the counter. He twirls a chain, tosses, but it comes crashing down. The men boo. Lucky tries again and the links clang over the crossbeam.

Ajax nudges me. "How much?"

"You mean, for my woman?"

"Yeah."

"Evo's not for sale."

"Everyone's for sale these days, lightweight."

Lucky searches for songs over at the jukebox. He fumbles a stack of 45s. The lone woman patron extinguishes her mini cigar on the jukebox hood and helps Lucky pick up records. She's wearing a black spider-webby dress and fishnet stockings.

The Nurse and the School Girl join Ajax. He pulls them close.

The French Maid comes over from the bar. Her nostrils are white with powder. She's having trouble striding the Berber on plexi pumps. She trips and I grab her. "Nice catch, honey," she goes. She towers over me and her laced brassiere's eye level. She rubs her thigh against my crotch. "Horny?"

"Sorry," I tell her, "I'm taken."

"Taken doesn't mean you can't play."

David Bowie whimpers over the speakers. Ajax tells the Nurse to put on something else. She joins Lucky and the woman at the jukebox. The French Maid takes her place beside Ajax. A needle scratches across a record and Ajax groans. The Violent Femmes start crooning, "Add It Up." Lucky bump-dances the woman and the Nurse.

Evo grabs the pole and dips. She slips off her halter. Her firm breasts push against a black bra. She unbuttons her cut-offs, kicks them across the counter, and catwalks in a black G-string. "Fuck me now," the Hell's Angel calls. The neon catches the curve of Evo's hips and rock-hard buns. She plucks a gold-studded black cap off the Hell's Angel, plops it on her own head, and tilts the brim.

"Show us your tits!" goes Ajax.

Evo unhooks her bra. Her breasts spring out—they seem to defy gravity as her nipples point up. She spreads the doubled-up chain and sits on the links. She kicks out her legs and begins to swing. The swings get longer and longer, until soon she's covering the entire counter. Her body glides through shadow and neon. The toughs stare in disbelief, as if an angel too sensual for crude remarks has appeared. She is the beauty most men dream about as boys, the one that made them believe in love and that fate or luck would deliver her to them. Evo's swings shorten. She pulls herself up and flies with her legs spread, as if they weren't legs at all but wings.

"Add It Up" goes into a final chorus and Evo pikes off the chain. She lands on the counter and the toughs reach up trying to touch her.

Ajax nudges me.

"She wet your whistle?" I ask.

"Premium," he says, "premium for the hottest fuckin' dancer west of Sin City."

RED RUM RIG

AJAX GAVE US two thumbs up. Lucky pumped gas from a barrel behind the warehouse while an armed bouncer looked on. The pigtailed Asian asked for "organics," so I traded the last of the 'shrooms for five cans of herring and a sack of fortune cookies. Now we're back in Rovy driving the Goleta shore. Sudzy's in the carrier on the floor mat. Cosmo gnaws a pig's ear in cargo—a gift from Lucky. The traffic's solar-powered micro cars, hybrids, and ten-speeds. The boardwalk's hopping with rollerblading babes and skateboarders. I feel re-energized with a full tank and hopeful we'll make it to Oregon. I look over at Evo. She stares at the road ahead with the sack of fortune cookies on her lap.

"Gimme a fortune," I go.

Evo pulls a cookie and cracks it. Cookie shards fall on her thighs as she unfurls the paper. "Foolish is the man who depends on the mercy of others," she tells me.

"Figures. I'm a magnet for the Fool Card."

"Foolish in love?"

"Fate smiled on me there, Babe."

We cruise by the palm entrance to a park. Most of the trunks are tagged. A lone chopper is parked in a sand pit with swings and a rusted slide. People gather around stoves and makeshift fires on the park grass. Gulls perch like vultures on trashcan rims.

"You saved us," I tell Evo.

She nibbles a cookie shard. "Hope I didn't hurt the baby."

"Any pain?"

"No."

"Our baby's fine," I reassure her.

*   *   *

The 101 twists northeast and the four-laner shrinks to a two-lane road. We enter a coastal prairie of sand dunes and chaparral. The wind hurls blasts of sand into Rovy. A motor home and a few tents squat on a saddle-like hump between dunes. The road swings west, returns to the coast. Evo spots a bouquet of red balloons floating in the clouds. I take the Pismo ramp and crush bone-white shells on the frontage road. I park. Cosmo leaps out when I swing open the cargo door. Evo harnesses Sudzy and walks her through freeway ice plant. The beach is deserted. The only sign of life is an outpost of pastel umbrellas, towels, and coolers.

Evo points south. "What's that, Tony?"

I spot the Kon Tiki Inn rising out of the sand. The tiled façade looks strangely Moorish with its curving archways and mini onion dome. "My old stomping grounds," I reply.

"Looks sketchy, Tone."

"Could be. Bring the shotgun."

We pill Sudzy and offer her canned tuna. She won't eat. We keep her in Rovy but don't stick her in the carrier.

Evo and I trek along the beachfront. Cosmo chases a gull. I've got Dave's binoculars hanging off a cord around my neck and the Beretta's in my shoulder holster. Evo cradles Super Shorty. It's nice having a wife who's armed and dangerous. We hop globs of oil and leap over fleshy strands of kelp. Strange things are entangled in the strands: a deflated sex doll, photos studded with barnacles, floats with Japanese symbols, and a dead sea turtle. Pelicans skim the sea. Ahead, the Pismo Pier looks like a child's dismantled Erector Set. Deck sections are missing, the anchoring posts lean, and the railings are gone.

We pass the Athletic Club. Its picture-frame windows are webbed with cracks. The tennis nets are gone and the lawn green courts I remember are now a mottled lime. Cosmo jogs the club's deck. I whistle him back. A breeze kicks up that feels like a blast of AC.

We reach the Kon Tiki. Dadio took me and Jimmy here the first summer of the twenty-first century, long before the rigs mushroomed offshore during the oil boom. The inn's southern wall is tagged RRR. I hear the distant beat of rockabilly and make out Jake Bugg singing,

"Lightning Bolt." The Kon Tiki beach is a dump of dinged-up boards, shattered flat screens, stained mattresses, and condoms. We head for the pool, passing a Jacuzzi of brown sludge and a railing with a display of rusted revolvers. I pick up a .44 and try rotating the cylinder—it won't budge.

Evo does the Triangle pose on the lip of the pool.

I join her. Weeds sprout in a bed of sparkling debris on the pool's bottom. The mosaic tiles that once adorned its sides lie broken below and the gutters are filled with bottle caps, cards, and bullet casings.

"How many stars?" Evo asks.

"For the inn?"

"Yes."

"Dadio gave it four out of five. Wanna grab a room?"

"No. But I've really gotta pee."

I spot a yellow Porto-Potty behind a line of outdoor grills. "There," I point.

Evo takes off and jams Super Shorty's barrel against the plastic door. It flies open.

I pee on a shrunken palm and look out to sea. Rigs squat in the mid-water between the breakers and the outer beds of kelp. The rigs bloomed when the oil quit flowing from the Middle East and gas reached $50-a-gallon. The President approved the leasing of vast expanses of coastal waters to big oil companies like Shell and BP for next to nothing. I zip up. One rig catches my eye. I return to the Jacuzzi and lift the binos—the red crane on its deck tilts precariously. Boats and skiffs are tethered to its steel legs. Two tugs and a yacht are moored there too. Rope ladders swing from the deck down to the sea. A swell lifts the hulls.

I lower the binos. The marine layer rolls in and the sun looks like the moon through the fog. It turns quiet. I can't hear Jake Bugg. It's that deadly silence before danger strikes. I hear a *humma-hum-hum* that sounds like a weed whacker and spot a gang of red jet skis cruising the shore, their engines shooting vertical streams of water. There are eight men on four jets. One jet lags. The driver in the lead jet raises his hand. All the jets except the lagger glide onto the beach. Cosmo scampers down to greet them. The men on the last jet leave it in the shallows.

"Evo," I call.

The men mill around the jets. One with a black eye patch pulls out a pocket telescope and studies me. "Friend or foe?" he calls up.

"Friend."

The men follow Eye Patch toward the Kon Tiki. Damn. I'm outnumbered again. Now I know why survivalists travel in packs. They surround the Jacuzzi and draw handguns from hip holsters. The only one without a gun is Eye Patch. Cosmo sniffs Eye Patch's trunks.

"Scouting for the PA?" Eye Patch asks me.

"No."

"Don't bullshit us," a man in a wetsuit snaps. "We've had reports."

"I'm just passing through," I tell them.

The wet-suited man mumbles something to Eye Patch.

"Where's home, amigo?" goes Eye Patch.

"Vista."

"In Cali?"

The pump action of a shotgun growls and Evo stands at my side holding Super Shorty. "We're San Diego County," she answers.

The sliders on seven semi-autos crank, sending bullets into the chambers. Evo aims at Eye Patch. A breeze rustles the dead fronds of a palm. I hear singing—it's faint at first but builds. A gravelly voice drifts out of the Kon Tiki and tumbles to the Jacuzzi. I hear Eric Burdon crooning "House of the Rising Sun." That song takes me back to Dadio's dusty LPs. "You guys Burdon fans?" I ask.

Eye Patch smiles. "All right, men," he says, "we've got us two Friendlies."

They holster their guns and Evo lowers her barrel.

Eye Patch extends his hand. "Paul Nolan," he tells me, "RRR."

We shake. "Tony Pernicano," I say. "This is Evo, my better half."

"What's RRR?" Evo asks.

"Red Rum Rig," the wet-suited man explains, "home sweet home, on the Great Rig of Total Defiance."

The introductions go around. The wet-suited man is Frank, second in command. Paul Nolan talks about the Phoenix Army's onslaught of the Coastal Townships and being forced into the ocean and onto the rig to escape waves of bloodthirsty warriors. Rigs became safe haven for refugees and soon rig colonies were established. The PA originated in Camp Fema Phoenix, and the core ranged from NRA survivalists to radical environmentalists to gung ho lesbians with hardcore combat training. The PA had a scorched earth policy so their leaders sent Black Hawks to destroy the rigs. Most became fireballs. The super rigs sustained damage but didn't buckle, thanks to BP, Chevron, and the other oil companies reinforcing them with titanium legs and tungsten hooks anchored a mile beneath the ocean floor. The PA rockets took out two of the RRR's legs but it didn't collapse. A winter storm hit. "The storm to end all storms," Paul said, one that turned back the PA's armada of assault rafts, power boats, and fishing vessels fitted with heavy artillery. Swells generated by a Hawaiian quake twisted the deck and a third leg buckled. The rig's western edge dipped twenty feet into the deep blue. The PA waited, but the storm raged on. Soldiers were needed for an uprising in Quadrant 5, so the PA retreated to Long Beach after enslaving captured women and girls. Men and boys weren't so lucky. If you were male, you got bused to the Rose Bowl and were forced to run a gauntlet of warriors. Blood, sweat, and piss flooded the stadium grass. Head pyramids grew as high as the goal posts.

A man in a World War I trench helmet, tie-dye shirt, and camouflage pants bounces out of the lobby. Silver hair spills out from beneath the helmet and he bare foots it around the pool swinging a boom box that plays, "We've Got To Get Out Of This Place." We all watch him jump over lounge chairs as if they were hurdles.

"Friend of yours?" Evo asks.

"Meet Weird Harold," Frank replies.

"Pismo native?" I go.

"Harold used to own the Kon Tiki," Paul answers.

I flash back to the good old days. I remember meeting the owner with Dadio. But that guy had a crew cut, bow tie, and white tennies.

"PA took Harold's family," Paul says. "Wife and three daughters."

"Not him?" I ask.

Frank winces. "He was hiding in a Porto-Potty."

Weird Harold does another lap, leaps over a carton of Pampers, and jogs back inside.

"That your Rover?" Paul asks me.

"Sure is."

"Gas in those cans on top?"

I can hear the waves breaking on the shore.

Frank clears his throat.

I look at Evo and she frowns.

"You guys need food," Paul tells me, "right?"

"What kinda food?"

He points at the sea. "See those floats?"

I notice a string of red floats bobbing outside the breakwater. "Lobs?" I ask.

"Knew you were a lobster man, Tony."

*   *   *

Evo runs back to check on Sudzy. The rig families float over on small boats and kayaks. I meet their wives and children. The elders stayed behind because the ladders were too risky.

I stroll the shore. A volleyball game begins near the Athletic Club, one that pits kids against adults. A man in a chef's hat fires up a grill on the club's deck. Frank sinks a bamboo pole with the RRR flag in the sand. A boy tosses Cosmo a Frisbee. A guard with a rifle is perched on a Kon Tiki veranda. The sky has a minty hue, the sign of an early autumn, one that reminds me we need to reach Crater Lake long before that first snow. Evo waves from the club and jogs down to join me. We hold hands and wade through the shallows. The

117

water's warm. Perch skitter by. I remember that first surf lesson I gave Evo in Carlsbad.

"Sudzy okay?" I ask her.

"The princess won't eat."

"Should we try lobster?"

Evo smiles big, revealing that sexy space between her front teeth. She's way too young for me, even though I'm only six years her senior. Still, sometimes I feel mega older, usually after I get winded or my ankles crack in bed.

"Chow time!" booms a megaphone.

Evo and I join the families on a deck lit by solar torches. Paul insists that we sit at his table. We dine on lobster off fine china and sip ice wine from Kon Tiki mugs. The wine's too sweet for me but Evo loves it. Paul snagged a case bottled in Iceland. It was a final harvest, the end result of plucking frozen grapes off Reykjavík vines.

Cosmo sniffs around the deck so I toss him a lobster tail. I look west and see white lights outlining the rig's crane. Paul wants us to stay. He says we'll be members of the Pacific Rig Colony, an alliance of thirteen rigs beginning at the Sea of Cortez, wrapping around Baja, and stretching north to Puget Sound. One is really an offshore city because it has ten rigs joined by steel bridges.

Feet scramble over the deck.

"Black Hawk!" warns the megaphone.

Frank races for the pole and tries signaling the rig by waving the flag.

I grab Evo's hand and we duck behind a brick wall. A helicopter *chop-chop-chops* from the south and flies over the Kon Tiki. Small caliber rounds from the guard sounds like a cap gun. The Black Hawk follows the coast north and looks like a shadow against the half-light of dusk. Paul fires a flare that hangs in the sky like a tiny sun. The crane's lights go out as the flare fades.

The Black Hawk veers west. A rocket from the rig scorches the sky with a red trail before falling harmlessly in the water. The Black Hawk closes in on the rig. A second rocket screams over our heads and a third nearly hits the Kon Tiki. The fourth rocket rips toward the Black Hawk. The helicopter explodes and fiery fragments scatter into the sea. A cheer goes up from the club. A return cheer comes from the rig.

Evo squeezes my hand. "Dine and dash?"

I nod. "The time to vamanos has arrived."

MALPASO RANCH

WE GO NORTH four miles to Shell Beach, where I pitch tent on a bluff. Stars blanket the heavens. A breeze off the Pacific rustles our tent. Evo, Sudzy, and Cosmo are safe inside. The Big Dipper hangs above Pismo. This new world can be so peaceful at times, but I know anything can happen. Oregon seems so far away that it feels impossible to reach. My hope is dwindling.

*　　　*　　　*

I fall asleep in Evo's arms and dream I'm bodysurfing at Pismo with Jimmy. I'm my age now but he's still a boy. I know he's Dadio's favorite, but I'm cool with that. Dadio spots a shark.

"Jimmy!"

"One more wave," Jimmy calls back. A triangle appears and tears through the surf. Jimmy vanishes and the day turns black. The Coast Guard floodlights the sea. I wake with a paralyzing sense of loss, the way I felt the day Jimmy died in the oil fields. That day destroyed my parents. I grieved with them for my lost brother, but there was nothing I could do to ease their pain.

*　　　*　　　*

Evo's starving at dawn. Me too. I break open the MREs and find potato cheddar soup, chicken with buffalo style sauce, and eggplant lasagna. At first I find it unappetizing squeezing food out of foil packs into plastic bowls, but we eat everything.

After breakfast, I start Rovy and we continue up PCH. I steer around a dead horse, and Evo makes the Sign of the Cross. I'm glad we've got gas, guns, ammo, and water. Evo holds Sudzy on her shoulder like a baby. The princess refused breakfast. She doesn't purr. She won't drink. I sweep a hand over her back and feel only fur and bone. "Not good," I grumble.

The highway curves around Morro Bay. Morro Rock offshore looks like the head of a sea monster. Swells roll over a milk-glass blue bay and slam into the Rock's craggy shore. Pelicans wing over the water.

We pass roadside trucks. Most of the beds are stacked with nets. A woman with a bucket hat sits on her tailgate threading a hook. A TUNA & PERCH sign is nailed to an ash tree. A tarp roof on posts shades aluminum pails buzzing with flies. A man kneels beside the pails tapping a gaff hook against his palm. I smell the stench of rotting fish. People stand in line with things to trade: bicycles, kayaks, rifles, and even a mink coat.

"Fresh fish?" I ask Evo.

"Don't stop, Tony. Don't stop for anything."

* * *

I drive until Evo spots the spires of Hearst Castle. Off-road is

121

dirty-blond sand with pines crowding the gorges. Clumps of roadside lupine shudder as we pass.

Evo taps my shoulder. "Pull over."

I turn into a rest stop. Evo strokes Sudzy on her lap. The princess goes rigid, her eyes rolling back in their sockets. All I see is white as her tail flicks wildly. The tail freezes, and Sudzy goes as limp as a rag doll.

"No," begs Evo, "not your time yet, princess." She cradles our cat like a child and weeps.

I stroke Evo's face and run my hand through her hair. "You were the best mother," I tell her but my words sound hollow.

She pulls out a peach half blanket and twines the fabric around Sudzy. I stare west. The sky looks over-exposed, the blue faded to a jaundiced yellow the way it gets in old pictures. I feel like a loser for not reaching Oregon by now. But what difference would it have made? Is dying in Oregon any easier?

I take Moonstone Road and turn Cosmo loose. Evo holds Sudzy and we follow a white sand path through a gorge with a tiny waterfall and bubbling stream. The stream feeds a small pool. There's a stone mound beside the pool. Wind whistles through the pines above us.

Evo puts the princess down beside the pool. "We need a ceremony, Tony."

"Dadio built funeral pyres."

"Will you build one?"

"Sure." I leave Evo and walk to the shore. Cosmo barks at the waves and runs into the surf. A wave crashes and rolls, soaking my bare feet. The shallows are green but it turns aquamarine farther out. The sky shifts back to blue. I find a stick and throw it for Cosmo.

I locate driftwood above a high tide mark speckled with shells. I stack the wood, find a length of nylon cord, and bundle it. I sling the bundle over my shoulder and head back. Evo's on the shoreline. She has her arms locked around her knees and she rocks back and forth while waves surge around her. Cosmo trots over and nudges her with his nose.

She pats him. "You're my best buddy, Cosmo."

"It's time," I tell her.

We return to the pool. I slip off the cord and separate the pine driftwood from the cedar. I weave the cedar branches together by crisscrossing them, making sure to tuck the verticals under and over the horizontals. I remember Dadio building a pyre for our lab and, after the small-branched web, he made the frame. I begin a pine frame but can't recall how Dadio kept the sections together. "Back in a flash," I tell Evo.

I return with the nail gun and a can of gas. I nail the pine branches together, forming what resembles the skeleton for a miniature hull. I tuck the cedar web into the pine frame so it's snug and place the cradle on top of the stone mound. Evo takes Sudzy out of the blanket. She puts her in the cradle and covers her body with orange poppies. I wet the corners of the pyre with gas and strike a match. The cradle ignites with a rush.

"Dear Lord," Evo says, "watch out for our princess in your Kingdom."

Smoke curls into the sky. I remember visiting Rancho Coastal and how we adopted a gray kitten after she stuck her paws through the bars to touch Evo. We rushed her to emergency because her spay wasn't done right. Her fur looked like it had been dipped in silver and, years later, we found out she was a Russian Blue.

I hug my woman as memories rush in. Evo seems numb, as if losing the animal she loved so hard pierced her soul. How do I comfort her? All I can do is hold her. I retreat to that secret room inside me, the place where I store sadness and deal with loss in my own fumbling way.

*   *   *

I take the highway northeast, stunned by our loss. Part of me doesn't care if we make it to Oregon. Somehow the humming tires make the journey seem pointless. Evo's slouched in her seat with her head resting on the window. I drive through foothills and paved-over washes that dip Rovy up and down. The shocks creak. We meander through hills without trees until the road hooks around a mountain and brings us back to the coast. I spot a priest shoveling. Behind him, a surfboard looks like a tombstone stuck nose-down in the sand.

*   *   *

The Monterey hills are covered with derricks, their arms frozen in stages of pump or plunge. A small company with a huge drill cut through Monterey's quartz crust and found an ocean of oil from Ukiah south to Santa Barbara. Companies left Texas to join a boom that rivaled the Gold Rush. It was even crazier than the mining frenzy that ensued after a kid stumbled upon lithium in the dried-up beds of the Salton Sea. The production surge in domestic oil killed the price of gas. But World War III, our undeclared war against the Asian Alliance, sent gas prices into the stratosphere.

*   *   *

Rovy crosses Rainbow Bridge near Carmel. A slipper moon glows in the north like an ornament. Steel cables from a cell tower hang in web-like strands. Evo has her eyes closed. Cosmo's asleep in the backseat. The land is bright with fields of orange poppies and wildflowers.

A woman with cropped hair stands on the ridge above us. More women join her. All wear fatigues. They start sprinting north single file along the ridge. They run with bows and crossbows. Packs bristle with the feathered ends of arrows. They stop where the ridge ends, and the bows rise.

"Jesus!" I say, jamming the pedal. Rovy swerves but I regain control. I hear a *thu-wunk* as an arrow busts into the glass panel on our roof. The glass splinters around the barb but the panel doesn't shatter. I hit 100 and don't slow down until we reach the city's welcome sign.

I pull over to inspect the damage. The arrow's in solid. Vice grip extraction could break the panel. I dig through cargo and find my cable cutters.

Evo finds a second arrow inches from the fuel cap door. "Why?" she asks.

"Those women were hungry." I snip off the fiberglass shafts and apply sealant around the barbs so water won't leak in.

"We could have given them MREs, Tony."

"They're hunters, Babe. They wanted fresh meat."

*   *   *

We pass Mission San Carlos. Boys chew gum beside an overturned truck. A girl sucks a lollipop. Hobos with bindle sticks thumb for rides. A truck flying the Dixie flag flickers its brake lights—it suddenly veers for the beach.

"What the fuck," I go.

"End of the road," says Evo.

A bus blocks PCH. Mannequins sit in the seats, their flesh-colored faces staring out. A plywood FREE FOOD sign is propped on an easel. A woman on the roof studies us through a telescope. A man cracks a whip against the side of the bus.

"Beach or forest?" I ask Evo.

"Forest."

I shift to 4WD and go off-road. We lurch up an incline of crumbling limestone, reach a plateau, and descend on a wetland.

Egrets flock. A big woman sits in a wicker throne on a dry patch between diverging streams. She's stirring a smoldering pot with a tire iron. "I'm Wendy," she blathers, "the Wicked Witch of Carmel!"

"Sayonara," I say and hit the gas.

We cross a stream and power through a stagnant pond. We reach the base of a second plateau. I downshift to first and Rovy's tires dig up the incline. We make the top and drop down again to the edge of a forest. Evo finds a path through the redwoods and I take it—it's just wide enough for Rovy. Branches drag over the fenders. Ferns, lilies of the valley, and grape vines carpet the dark forest floor. Cowboys on Appaloosas trot by. I follow them over a wooden bridge and the slats creak beneath us.

"There," Evo says, pointing to a plywood shack.

I pull alongside a shack with FRESH PRODUCE painted in green on its side. A blue Jeep Cherokee is parked beside a stack of crates near the door. We get out. Evo does the Half Moon pose. I stretch and crack my window for Cosmo. Evo snaps on her fanny pack, and we walk past a compost heap. I swing open the screen door and we enter a store with a hay floor. Thatched baskets overflow with peaches, apricots, grapefruit, and oranges. The citrus smell makes the shack seem friendly. Pictures of women wearing headscarves are taped to the wall. "Snoods," Evo whispers. There are photos of children too, and all wear headbands. Evo sniffs an orange. Kale, zucchini, tomatoes, and arugula are in the veggie section. Rosemary, sage, cilantro, and basil are bunched with rubber bands. Evo tells me they've run out of avocados.

I find a bin of husked coconuts. I pick one up, shake it, and it gurgles with milk. "A+ survival," I tell Evo.

"How's that, Tone?"

"Coconuts are packed with vitamins. Plus, they'll keep for months."

"I've gotta lovely buncha coconuts," comes a voice.

A man with a red beard wanders over, his leather sandals slapping on the hay. His shirt and pants are burlap. He even has a burlap headband. "Welcome to the Farmstand, friends," he says, "I'm Uriel."

"Tony," I tell him, "and this is my wife, Evo."

"Ah," he sighs, "First Woman."

"Any pesticides?" Evo asks.

"Chemicals are forbidden here. Malpaso's 100% organic."

I pull an ounce of silver bullion from my pocket. "Will this work?"

Uriel purses his lips. "Either that or gold. The Master prefers gold, but that's not important. The important thing is guiding you to His righteous path. You gentle folk from Carmel?"

"San Diego," I reply.

"Salt of the earth down south."

"Any more avos?" asks Evo.

"God is my light," smiles Uriel.

"Huh?" I go.

Uriel snatches hay off a bale and scatters it over a patch of dirt. "We do have avos," he says, "but not here. Come to Malpaso with me and you can pick as many as you need. No charge. Our ranch was once Clint Eastwood's gentleman estate."

"The Good, the Bad, and the Ugly," I say.

Uriel makes a gun with his thumb and index finger and sights down the barrel. "King of the Spaghetti Westerns."

"Is Eastwood dead?" Evo asks.

"The Lake of Fire," Uriel answers. "Now, if you folks would be so kind as to follow my Jeep."

"Great," I say. "But who's minding the store?"

He nods at the veggie section. "Roah."

I see a heavyset snood stuffing baskets with fresh bunches.

Evo fills a crate with fruit. I toss Uriel the bullion and we follow him out. He gets in the Cherokee. I start up Rovy and shadow him as he drives on the pitted shoulder. Emerald hills to the north erupt from burnt-yellow fields. Cowboys thread their horses through the redwoods below us. I imagine Clint in a movie on a molten shore, one where the devil invites him out of a bar at high noon. Clint has a shot of whiskey and struts barefoot down Main Street. He has no gun. The devil draws and fires six times. Clint waves his hand, transforming the bullets into butterflies. "That the best you got, pardner?" goes Clint.

Uriel hangs a right off the shoulder. I follow him over a dirt road with dips and wicked divots. I look through my wing mirror— the highway's hidden behind a fringe of tall sour grass. I hit a divot and the springs groan. I hate the idea of a stranger leading us through a farm tucked behind the main road. But Uriel seems harmless. I mean, how dangerous could a bearded man in sandals be?

"Uriel's an odd name," I tell Evo.

"Old Testament."

"Eye for an eye?"

"Tooth for a tooth."

"What's the Lake of Fire?"

"Maybe a new resort in Vegas."

The Cherokee speeds up. I shift to third and hit the gas.

"And who the hell's 'The Master?'" I ask.

"Someone to avoid," Evo advises. She reaches back and pats Cosmo.

"Could their leader be a woman?"

"No way. Women in the Old Testament were treated like

slaves."

We reach a gate held open with cinder blocks. The gate's scripted MALPASO RANCH letters and silhouette horse head logo are frosted with rust. We enter a junkyard of stripped cars and trucks. Scotch thistle weeds thrive on the roadway, their purple flowers sending out thorny pods. Cicadas chirp. Skeleton weed pokes through the spokes of a wagon wheel. A longhorn's skull and horns rest on the arm of a saguaro. Dragonflies hover over Rovy's hood. A wasp stings the windshield.

"Wild West theme," I tell Evo.

"Think Clint's still alive?"

"Bet that old fart's holed up in the Coliseum."

I smell the wild aroma of lantana. Bushes of blooming lantana appear and hummingbirds suck the flowers. Evo sticks bare legs through her open window. She reminds me of a teenager on her first cross-country adventure.

Evo wiggles her toes. "Is this a trap, Tony?"

"Sure, Babe. Maybe a forced Bible study."

"Or a stoning."

"Very funny."

We follow Uriel through a dried-up riverbed with banks of salt cedar. The sun glares off our hood as we cross the bed and climb a hill. We enter a lavender meadow with bees swarming the blossoms.

A barn looms in the distance, and a hot house is plopped at the base of a hill. We reach a pasture of fenced-in animals. Sheep flick their tails as we pass. A billy stands on his hind legs and nibbles persimmon leaves. A brown cow waddles the fence line, her belly swollen with a calf. The road becomes crushed coral. The Cherokee's tires kick up puffs of white dust that fly through our windows like smoke. The road skirts an avo grove and stretches up to the hot house.

Uriel leaves the coral road and zips over a stretch of grass with walking paths. He pulls up to a red ranch house with dormer windows. A snood stands in the doorway rocking a baby. Behind her, girls load a washing machine. I park beside Uriel under a peppercorn tree. Cosmo leaps over my lap when I open my door. Evo whistles but Cosmo darts past the tree and races toward a lake.

Evo pulls on her sneakers. "I'll go get him," she says.

Uriel slides crates out of the Cherokee and I help. We stack the crates under the tree. He lifts his hood and pulls the dipstick.

"Okay for our dog to run around?" I ask.

Uriel wipes the dipstick with his fingers. "You're our guests," he replies.

Beside the ranch house, snoods hang clothes on a line. Children sit under an ancient oak listening to a snood read. Bearded men, all with their hair pulled back and knotted, load a flat bed. A girl with raven hair cries as she runs past the peppercorn to a brick well. A snood jogs over and hugs her.

Uriel slams his hood. "Stay as long as you like," he tells me.

"How long is long?"

"Take the sacred oath, and stay till the Day of Judgment." Uriel tells me how to reach the avocado grove and heads into the house.

I join Evo at the lake. Cosmo barks at the ducks. The water's clear and clean. Water flows into the lake through white pipes on the opposite shore. A man in a blue robe stands beside the pipes staring at us. I wave. He doesn't wave back.

*   *   *

The sun breaks over the eastern hills. Cotton-candy clouds drift by. Evo's in her cut-offs on a ladder beside an avocado tree. She reminds me of a farm girl at harvest time, a cutie with apple cheeks and long legs. I raise a wooden bucket. Evo drops in a handful. Cosmo runs along the row of trees. Before harvesting, we drove down the coral road and watched men pack hydroponic lettuce beside the hot house. Boys helped—they reminded me more of little men than kids. Cosmo tried making friends, but Roah shooed him away. We parked here in the grove and I pulled out the folding ladder a snood named Judith gave us.

Evo descends the ladder. She pulls her Swiss Army knife and slices an avocado. She balances a sliver on the blade.

I pluck it off and munch. "Delicioso."

She cuts herself a slice. "Let's stay for the wedding."

"What wedding?"

"The festivities are two days off. Judith told me about it."

"No way."

"C'mon, it'll be fun. Besides, we need a break from the road. Our baby does too."

"All right," I give in. "But don't get too cozy."

"Our hosts are cool, don't you think?"

"I guess."

"I've been thinking, Tony."

Uh, oh, I think. Here it comes.

"What if we had our baby here? Judith's a midwife and Uriel's almost a vet."

"Sterling credentials," I mumble.

"Don't you see, Tony? I'd be safe. Judith has a birthing kit and everything."

"We'll miss our window."

"Well, think about it."

"Okay," I moan. I picture Evo in a snood, me sprouting a beard, and Cosmo harnessed to a cart pulling oranges out to the Farmstand.

*　　　*　　　*

Uriel invites us to dinner during a sunset flurry of avo picking.

We thank him and he walks off down the coral road. What I really want is to be alone with my woman but we haven't had a serious meal since the lobs at Pismo. I pull off my shoulder holster and Beretta and stash them in Rovy. I take Evo's hand and we stroll to the coral road. The sky's purple. It's the time of in-betweens. We leave the road, take a gravel path past the well, and arrive at the ranch house. Lanterns light the base of the peppercorn tree. Men are hunkered down on chairs under the tree. Snoods flit over from the house carrying ceramic plates loaded with mullet fillets, corn, and beans. One snood carries mugs filled with wine. The women are the waitresses and they rarely speak. The children aren't here. Judith, a lanky snood with blue eyes, finds us seats next to Uriel and a wizened man named Isaac. Roah brings us plates piled high with food.

"Where's the Big Kahuna?" I ask.

Isaac grimaces. "The Master returns from the Carolinas tomorrow," he says.

After dinner, Uriel plucks a banjo. Roah clangs a tambourine. A fiddle joins in. Everyone stands, joins hands, and hums. Judith coaxes us to hum along. The humming becomes a chorus and soon I'm singing my praises to someone named "Yashua." The song ends, and that's followed by a celebration of hoots and claps. The men mingle outside the ranch house while the snoods clear the plates and mugs.

"Hey, Tone," whispers Evo, "if the women are snoods, what do we call the men?"

"I don't know. Any suggestions?".

"Beards."

"I can go for that," I tell her.

THE WEDDING

THE MARINE LAYER rolls in off the ocean and cools Malpaso. I stand beside the balloon frame of a house. Beards pull a glinting white sheet of satin over the skeleton roof. SHABBAT is stitched in purple on the satin. Uriel and Isaac place wooden tiles for the floor. More beards arrive toting a floral loveseat, copper candleholders, and an assortment of flutes, fiddles, and guitars. I think of the Seven Dwarfs, only these guys are taller and there are more of them.

Evo's not here. She's making lamb sandwiches and leek soup over at the ranch house. She felt guilty after Judith brought breakfast to the barn. We slept well last night on canvas cots. There were no horses or cows in the barn. Not even a cat. Instead, the barn's filled with muscle cars from the Seventies, including a blue Cuda, a Shelby Cobra, and a Pantera.

A flatbed pulls up. A beard in a blue robe gets out. "Remember our deadline," he coaches. Beards slide tables and chairs off his flatbed. He ambles toward me and we watch them unload. The lines in his forehead go deep, and his face is dark from the sun. Leather bands wrap around his forearms.

"Big night tonight," I say.

He keeps his eyes on the workers. "Yes."

"This a Jewish shindig?"

He turns. His eyes are so brown they're nearly black. A silver bar dangles off a chain around his neck. The Ten Commandments are engraved on twin tablets in the silver. "Stranger," he scowls, "do I know you?"

"No."

"Have we broken bread?"

"Not yet," I go, holding out my hand. "I'm Tony."

We shake. His fingers and palm are heavy with calluses. "Abraham," he tells me.

"The Master?"

He releases my hand. "Never call me that," he warns, "unless you're family." Abraham returns his attention to the work. He whistles and points at the truck. Isaac rushes over and lifts poles off the flatbed. "Had a half-brother named Tony," he says, "in another life."

"You're my first Abraham."

He points at the lake. "Is that your beast, Tony?"

I spot Cosmo—he's chasing a duck through the reeds. "Yes," I reply.

"And is that your arrowed Rover parked in the grove?"

"Uh, huh."

He adjusts his headband. "You crossed paths with the Archery Club, a female militia rooted in barbarism and a shared hatred of men. Those harlots will devour anything with hair on it."

"Guess I was lucky."

"Stay with us, Tony. You, First Woman, and your daughter-to-be. You'll be safe at Malpaso. Come with me, I want to show you something."

I follow Abraham as he hustles by the Shabbat and strides up a hill. The soil is red and pitted with holes. I wonder how he knows our baby will be a girl. We pass outhouses, a diesel generator, and a dump. Abraham plucks a blossom off a jacaranda. Coconut shells with painted faces hang off the tree's limbs. Most have expressions of fear and suffering. Some depict death, with Xed out eyes and flatline lips. A crow lands in the tree. A breeze kicks up. The faces make hollow sounds as they clink together.

"Some tree," I tell him.

"The Enemy Tree, Tony."

"There must be a hundred coconuts."

"63."

"Is this voodoo?"

"No. Each nut represents an enemy of Malpaso, past and present. These are the ones who took it upon themselves to foster personal gains or to satisfy sexual cravings and other immoralities. Only a handful still breathe."

"You kill 'em?"

Abraham clears his throat. "These degenerates doomed themselves by ignoring their moral compasses and allowing demons to enter their souls. They are the filthy and the unjust. One was a lawyer who convinced a jury to free a murderer. Another a sexual fiend seducing boys. A third was a woman making the beast with two backs with her sister's husband. All broke sacred covenants and thus, will share the same eternal destiny on the Lake of Fire."

"No fun in that," I go.

"See that face on the highest branch, the one with slits for eyes?"

I spot it. The eyes have a matching slit for the mouth. "Super bad guy?"

"Jedediah the Traitor," he proclaims. "We took that destitute in because he was starving and without shelter. But he soon denounced us, after meeting a whore who convinced him to steal from Malpaso. Jedediah will reap what he has sowed."

I sense no forgiveness in him. Abraham lives in a black-and-white world, one with no middle ground between pure evil and absolute goodness. He could be your best friend one day and your mortal enemy the next. "Is Jedediah in our midst?" I ask.

"No."

"He's a goner?"

"Are you passing through, Tony?"

"Yes."

"May I ask your destination?"

"Oregon."

"Why the Northern Territories?"

"Water."

Abraham's forehead crinkles. His blue robe turns purple in a blast of sunlight. "I have a dozen wells," he says, "with 10,000 gallons stored."

"Water's not our only reason," I admit. "We want to return to nature and strike out on our own."

"Be careful, Tony. The northern highways are blocked. The roads are filled with murderers, rapists, and thieves. Never take First Woman and your unborn child there."

"We'll take our chances."

Abraham strokes his beard. "I admire courage. But in you I see foolishness springing from selfish pride, a flaw that will deliver you to death's door. The fate of your family hangs in the balance, Tony. Now if you will excuse me, I must return to the Shabbat. Will you and First Woman be joining us in celebration?"

"You can count on it."

"Until the wedding," Abraham bows, "shalom."

I watch him walk past the dump, the generator, and the outhouses. The marine layer returns. The coconut shells clink.

*   *   *

Evo and I are outside the Shabbat. The satin roof rustles. It's a good fit but it does hang low on the lake side. I'm in khaki Dockers and an aloha shirt. Evo looks fine in her mint top and white taffeta skirt.

THE NEW JERUSALEM and CITY OF PEACE banners hang from the skeleton frame inside. The wooden floor gleams. The central marble table has a silver goblet perched on it, and candles flicker on either end. Benches radiate out from the table. Beards and snoods crowd the benches. Children sit on chairs out on the lawn. A snood shaped like a plum grumbles whenever a boy or girl speaks.

A couple wearing white linen enters the Shabbat. They stand beside the floral loveseat. The groom's shirttails hang over his pants. His bride wears a yellow shawl and a violet-and-rose corsage. Her brown hair is braided with fern sprigs and purple ribbon. Her hem brushes the floor.

Roah and Judith join the bride and groom. Judith tells the bride that she is "worthy of the groom" because she overcame her enemies. Roah mixes passages from The Old Testament with womanly duties. "She wants to be what you need her to be," Roah tells the groom. "She's made herself vulnerable to you," coos Judith.

"She needs you for security," Roah adds. Judith says the loveseat is their throne and symbolic of the one Yashua sits on while ruling "the Eternal Universe."

"Bring me the crown!" bellows the groom.

A girl in a pink gingham dress carries a crown of white carnations forward. Her face shines like alabaster, and her black hair cascades over her shoulders. She's the one I saw crying the day we arrived. The girl kneels at the groom's feet and hands it to him. He places the crown on his bride's head.

Abraham arrives wearing a white robe with a red sash. He walks over to the couple, kisses the bride's cheek, and tells the couple to sit. They take the loveseat. Flutes and fiddles play. A tambourine joins in.

Abraham stands behind the altar. He closes his eyes and raises his arms over his head. "Let us celebrate this holy union," he says, "let us never forget this most righteous of days."

Drums pound, and that's followed by an avalanche of *whoo-hoo-hoos* and vigorous clapping. Corks pop. Snoods and beards mingle as glasses fill with wine. A handful of children enter the Shabbat. I want them to play with Cosmo, but remember I locked him in a paddock for safety. There are over two hundred guests, many without beards or snoods. Are they from neighboring villages? There were buses and motor coaches parked on the coral road.

Judith's hanging out with the crown girl on the lake side of the Shabbat. She lifts a wine bottle and motions for us.

"Time to socialize," Evo tells me.

She tugs me by the hand, and we weave through the crowd. I accidentally bump Isaac, and his wine goes flying. "Sorry, brother," I tell him. We reach Judith and she hugs Evo.

"I'm so glad you're here," Judith says. She hands us glasses and splashes in wine. "Mazel tov," she toasts and we all clink glasses.

The crown girl frowns as she sips from a plastic cup.

"Bored?" I ask her.

"Very," she answers, her eyes darting to the altar.

Abraham pours wine into the silver goblet. He meanders through the throng offering the goblet to guests. He ends his journey at Evo's side.

"Will you drink, First Woman?" he asks.

Evo places her lips on the goblet's rim. Abraham tilts. Wine spills out of the corners of Evo's mouth and splashes her mint top.

"May I taste the blessed wine, Master?" Judith asks.

"No, Judith. Not today."

"Isn't this a celebration?" I ask.

Abraham frowns. "Judith has disappointed me and, in so doing, has offended Yashua."

Judith grabs the crown girl's hand. They leave the Shabbat.

Abraham watches them march away over the lawn.

*   *   *

Guests stream into the fern grotto behind the ranch house and gather around a wooden platform. I lost Evo after she left to search for Judith. Beards string up a banner between two junipers. The banner announces THE END OF CIVILIZATION & THE DAWN OF A NEW AGE. I spot Evo—she's sitting on the edge of the platform. I head over. Poles with red flags are stuck in a Lazy Susan-type spinner nailed to the plywood floor. Each flag has a word in black: REBELLION, SELFISHNESS, IMMORALITY, SLANDER, SLOTH, GREED, ARROGANCE, and HATRED. I squeeze through a group of snoods and reach Evo.

"Find Judith?" I ask her.

"No." She holds out her hand and I pull her up.

Guests chatter around the platform. Men without beards have holstered side arms. Snoods and beards link hands and rock. The red flags begin to rotate—they spin slowly at first but soon are moving fast enough to blur the words.

A white robe floats ghostlike through the ferns—it's Abraham. He ducks under the banner and steps up on the platform. The flags slow. "Shalom," he bows.

"Shalom," the guests respond.

The flags stop.

"Friends and family," Abraham says, "a man can't be measured by his money, power, or knowledge. The true test of his greatness is his ability to love. We are all born free. Each of us is free to choose his or her own path, one that will determine whether you become the Filthy, the Righteous, or the Holy. As part of our family you are placed on the righteous path and guided toward salvation. Most outside Malpaso will suffer the fate of the Filthy and be vanquished. In these days and nights we fight for survival. Let us not forget that life is more than the survival of the body. It is also, and more importantly, the survival of the soul. Suppose a stranger offers you bread and water to nourish your body. This seems a holy act. But what good is it if he, in so doing, seeks to corrupt your morality? What good are you if robbed of your spiritual light? I say, refuse the stranger's offer. It is better to starve the body than to be seduced into losing your soul. No one escapes Judgment Day. I pray that our newlyweds today find eternal salvation and join the ranks of the Holy. Shalom."

"Shalom!" go the guests.

Isaac strums an acoustic guitar. A harp and fiddles join in. Roah grabs my hand while Uriel takes Evo's. They pull us into a big human chain and soon I'm circling with Evo around the platform singing:

The wrath of God has come to all his enemies.

The bowls are spilled as the trumpet sounds.

Yashua, Messiah, has won the victory!

The bride and groom join Abraham. She tosses her crown and a snood snags it. The music ends and the human chain breaks. Abraham invites everyone to the ranch house for dinner. A few trail after the newlyweds on their stroll back to the Shabbat for pictures. Two beards play fiddles. Snoods pluck the flags off the spinner.

"Hungry?" Evo asks.

"Always," I go.

I take her hand and we head for the ranch house. Solar lamps light the path from the grotto to the peppercorn tree. Guests squeeze through the front door of the ranch house with plates piled high. Evo and I slip in. Roah shouts in the kitchen. Beards lug stainless steel servers through the foyer. Another beard tinkers with the breaker box. We enter a main room accented with basket lampshades and macramé-and-bead curtains. Cowhide-covered benches line the far wall. Birch tables are etched with sheep, goats, and grape clusters. Murals that seem Biblical depict bygone days: men with droopy faces sit around a campfire; couples stand beside a pyramid of harvested wheat; a rag family plucks oranges near a crimson sea.

We join a line curving around the room. Slabs of lamb and fish fillets are stacked like pancakes in servers. Pitchers of lemonade glisten on a dolly. I snatch ceramic plates and bowls. We're behind a woman with granny glasses and a chubby man with a white goatee. It seems strange at Malpaso to see someone with shaped facial hair. He stabs a fillet and flops it on his plate.

"Yum," goes Evo, "that looks good."

The goatee man turns. "They use organic flour," he tells us.

Evo plucks corn off a platter. "Organic or nothing for me."

"Smart gal," the man says.

I nudge Evo. "That girl with Judith," I go, "was that her daughter?"

Evo dips a wooden ladle into a copper cistern of bubbling lentil soup. "Yes," she tells me, "that was Sarah."

"Who's her father?"

Evo motions for the bowls. I hand them over and she ladles in soup. She sticks a bowl on my plate. I heap on a bed of brown rice, lamb, and dollops of mint jelly. I wrap lamb in a napkin and stuff it in my pocket for Cosmo. I follow Evo out. We sit cross-legged on the grass under the peppercorn. The goatee man and his woman sit on a bench nearby.

"Malpaso resident or guest?" I ask him.

"Guest," he answers, "from Big Sur Township. We received a wedding invite so here we are."

"Does Abraham want you to join?"

"Sure does. But we're not fit for commune life, you know, living with religious types and their rules. It's okay for some but not for us. That said, forming allegiances is as healthy as organic flour. Am I right, Marge?"

"Right on the money, Hiram," the woman with granny glasses answers.

We chat about what happened to the coast, from Big Sur north to Mendocino. Hiram tells us the PA met little resistance crossing into Oregon, after ravaging the coastal cities and towns along the way. Locals at Big Sur retreated five miles inland and set up shop in a hidden valley, one with a small river and plenty of space for crops. "Banner year for white corn," Hiram boasts, telling Evo the corn she's munching came from his valley. Turns out Malpaso and the Big Sur Township have crop exchanges and share info about mutual enemies.

"You share guns?" I ask him.

"No. And we never intend to."

The newlyweds jog by, followed by beards playing fiddles and a boy on harmonica. The groom carries his bride over the doorstep to wild applause and the music continues inside.

We finish our meals. Evo sneaks off and returns with four plates of guava wedding cake. After dessert, Hiram pulls out a pocket watch and sticks it under a solar lamp beside his bench. He says it's time to round up their "contingency" from Big Sur.

Evo and I say our goodbyes as Hiram and Marge stroll off hand-in-hand.

"Wait here," Evo tells me. She makes a beeline for the Shabbat and returns with a bottle of merlot. We follow the lamps back to the barn. I unlatch a paddock door and Cosmo charges out.

"Feast, boy, feast," I say, tossing him meat.

Evo and I swig merlot out of the bottle. We find a spot below the hay chute and make one big bed out of four cots. Cosmo hunkers down on the hay. I lie beside Evo. I'm stuffed and woozy from wine. It feels great lying with the woman I love. Malpaso is a good place. We won't join, but this was a nice stop on the way to Oregon. I flash to Abraham in his white robe, and a creepy feeling overtakes me. "You sure were chummy with The Master," I tell Evo.

"So?"

"You hung out before the wedding?"

"We shared some port over at his cottage."

"What cottage?"

"Near the lake, silly boy. Tucked behind the reeds. Abraham says I have a chance."

"Chance for what?"

"Redemption."

"I suppose I'm one of the Filthy."

She giggles. "In spades."

"I get the Lake of Fire?"

"A one way ticket to Hell."

"Any conjugal visits?"

"Not a chance, hotshot. As the Filthy, you suffer alone for

Eternity."

"Can I fish that lake?"

"Teaming with devilfish," Evo replies. "Abraham reminds me of Charlton Heston in *The Ten Commandments*. Great Grams watched him religiously every Easter."

"My women ancestors lusted after Tom Jones."

"Ah, yes, Tom Jones. The root of all evil."

"Now headlining at the Beelzebub Hilton," I quip.

Evo clears her throat. "I want to get serious, Tone."

Uh, oh, I think, here we go.

She confesses she told Judith we were leaving for Oregon. Judith wants to leave with us and bring Sarah, but she's terrified Abraham will hurt her if he finds out. Evo promised Judith they could go, and that we'd leave at night after everyone fell asleep. "Does tomorrow work?" Evo asks.

"The sooner," I reply, "the better."

*   *   *

It's late morning. The sun has burned through the marine layer. Evo looks sexy picking apricots on the ladder. She's got on plaid shorts and a gray crop top. I don't know where she's getting all these clothes. She must have snuck in an extra suitcase back at Portico. I'm reading *The Waste Land* in the shade while Cosmo naps on a patch of clover. This was the first morning Roah didn't bring breakfast to the barn. No fresh eggs and sausage. No biscuits drowning in gravy. No O. J.

I hear the *clumpity-clump-clump* of boots.

"Over here!" a man says.

I lower my book. Abraham stands beside the ladder, his forearm resting on a middle rung. Uriel and Isaac are with him. More beards arrive, all wearing combat boots and jeans. Three have rifles.

Abraham taps the wooden rung with his fingernails. "Tony and First Woman," he says, "nice day for apricots."

"And reading poetry," I respond.

"I trust you had a righteous time at the wedding?"

"Yes. My compliments to all your musicians and chefs."

Abraham gazes up. His eyebrows squirm like caterpillars as he eyeballs Evo. "I'll tell the family you enjoyed our festivities," he says. "Time to descend your ladder, First Woman. Time for Tony to put away his poetry. You two will be coming with me."

I close the book and stand. "Where we going?"

"A place you can no longer corrupt others with your rebellious plans."

Evo hops off the ladder, brushes back her hair, and crosses her arms. "Abraham," she goes, "are you bummed I left the cottage too soon?"

"No. Judith told me about your plans to abduct her and Sarah, and flee for the Northern Territories."

"Judith wants to go."

Uriel and Isaac sneak closer to me. Another beard crab-walks under the apricot.

Cosmo gets up and growls.

Abraham plucks an apricot off a low branch. "Tony threatened to kill Judith if she didn't run away with him."

"Bull," I go.

"Listen, Abraham," Evo says, "Judith begged me for a ride. Tony made zero threats. Why don't you believe us?"

"Judith never lies. If she did beg as you say, why did you not tell me her desires? That shows your deceitful nature, First Woman. Maybe, given time, you will find salvation. Yashua can forgive those who have strayed."

"Time to split this nut farm," I tell Evo.

Abraham tosses the apricot and raises a hand. "That's no longer an option, Tony."

"No?"

"No. The gate has closed."

I grab Evo's hand and pull her down the row. Cosmo runs with us. Boots pound behind us. I tug Evo under a tree.

"There!" Uriel says.

I brush aside branches and we dodge the trunk. If we can just make that coral road we have a chance. We scramble through more trees and are forced to crawl when the trees get too small. We scoot under the last apricot tree and charge up an embankment. My shoes get coated in white dust topside. "This way," I tell Evo. We sprint over the coral with Cosmo at our heels. I spot white paint through the avocado trees. We zip into the grove and reach Rovy. Uriel's leaning against the hood. Beards with rifles squat on the back bumper.

"You're going nowhere," Uriel smirks.

"Okay, guys," I say, "you win."

Cosmo snarls, flashing his fangs.

I stomp my high-tops. "Run, Cosmo, run!"

Cosmo dodges Uriel. A beard raises his rifle but Cosmo scampers under a tree.

"Attaboy, Cosmo!" Evo goes.

"Your beast will be mine soon enough," Uriel says, "when he slinks on his belly begging for scraps. He will receive more than scraps from me."

I clench my fists. "You bastard."

"Cool head, Tony," Evo warns.

Uriel and the beards escort us back to the barn. Abraham opens a paddock and we're forced in at gunpoint. The door slams shut. The metal latch outside clinks into place. We're prisoners. Two folded cots are perched on a bale and a copper cistern's brimming with water. A tiny window high on the wall is covered with a mesh of chicken wire. Evo unfolds the cots. I tumble the bale over to the wall, stand on it, and look through the window. Flowerbeds extend from the outer wall to the well. Children sit under the oak as a snood paces. Abraham and Uriel march to the well and Abraham passes him an olive-green ammo can.

I pray for Cosmo.

I pray he runs far away and never returns.

CAPTIVES

EVO'S DOING the Eagle pose. A rooster crows. The aroma of fried eggs and sausage drifts into our cell through the tiny window. Roah slides aluminum trays under our door at dawn—we get mush and burnt toast. The cistern water tastes like sulfur. We've been in hell three days now. I tell jokes to pass the time. The bale's still under the window, and I stand on it to scout. No sign of Cosmo. I'm not sure what Abraham has planned, but I know he wants Evo. That means sayonara for me. I climb the bale and watch a snood shovel manure into a bed of daffodils. She spreads it with a hoe. I spot Sarah near the well. She throws a ball and a dog chases it over the lawn.

"Cosmo!" I go.

Evo breaks pose. "Where?"

"With Sarah."

Cosmo fetches and returns the ball to Sarah. She kneels and pats him. A beard approaches twirling a lasso. It's Uriel. Sarah waves him away, but he keeps coming.

"Run," I call, "run, Cosmo!"

Uriel tosses. The lasso grazes Cosmo's snout. He races by Uriel and sprints across the grass for the lake.

*   *   *

Evo's doing a headstand. She can slip into a trance and stand on her head for hours. Roah gave us a portable toilet but I find it embarrassing taking turns this close. Evo exits her trance and tumbles over. She starts rooting through the hay. She uncovers a Bratz doll, a toothbrush, and a picture of a blonde holding a baby.

"That's Judith," goes Evo.

"With Sarah?" I ask.

"Yes."

"Were they prisoners once?"

"All of Malpaso's a prison," Evo says.

*   *   *

On day seven, we're starving. No breakfast. No lunch. The cistern's empty. 2:15 on my wristwatch. I've been on my cot all day. Evo doing the Dead Body pose on the ground. I've grown bored spying out the window watching beards head from the ranch house over to the groves and snoods working the flowerbeds. Isaac draws water from the well at noon and trucks rumble over the lawn all day with crates. They congregate around the peppercorn at dinnertime and break out the fiddles.

"Evo?" comes a woman's voice. "Tony?"

At first I think I'm hallucinating. But the calling continues. I hop up on the bale and peer out the window.

Judith has her nose pressed against the chicken wire. She's tiptoeing on a stack of crates in the flowerbed. "Tonight we flee Galilee," she tells me. "Be ready."

*   *   *

The paddock door springs open at dusk. Uriel stands in the doorway holding a kerosene lamp. Beards with rifles stand behind him. "Hello, friends," he says. He passes Evo a basket. "Fish and unleavened bread for our sinners," he tells us.

"Where's Cosmo?" I ask.

"Gone."

"Gone where?"

"The Master never approved of unproductive beasts running free. Cosmo has gone to a better place."

"What better place?"

"I chased him down to the highway in the Jeep."

"You sonuvabitch."

"Roah's making your coconut, Tony," Uriel goes, "for the Enemy Tree."

"Great. Does Evo get one too?"

"Malpaso has plans for First Woman."

"What plans?"

Uriel smiles and shuts the door. The outside latch clicks into place.

"We're doomed," I say.

Evo pulls a mullet fillet from the basket. "We're not doomed," she says, "and I swear, we'll find Cosmo."

* * *

The night is pitch black. I stand on the bale looking through the window while Evo rests on her cot. The gathering for dinner over at the ranch house ended hours ago. This was their first night without fiddles. I have a feeling Abraham isn't at Malpaso, that he's off supervising satellite communes. No moon tonight. Even the stars are hard to see. I whistle for Cosmo. I imagine him hurt on the side of the road.

"Tone," Evo calls from the dark.

"What?"

"Visitors."

I hear footsteps and hop off the bale.

Someone's fumbling with the outside latch. The door creaks open and a flashlight beam blinds me. It's Judith, and Sarah's with her. Sarah's clutching a folded up quilt. "Here," goes Judith, handing me my keys.

"How'd you get these?" I ask.

"No time to explain." She's clutching the handle of a small suitcase and pushes back the front of her snood. "Can we go with you?"

"Of course," says Evo.

"Where's Abraham?" I ask.

"In a distant land."

Judith gives me the flashlight and I lead the way out of the barn. We pass the flowerbeds and the well. Even though we're hustling it feels like we're moving in slow motion. We slink through the apricots down to the coral road. Lights from the hot house twinkle on the hillside. We jog the coral until the first avocado tree appears and I count the lead trees until we reach the third row. I spot white paint through the branches.

"This way," I tell them.

The gas cans are still strapped to Rovy's roof. Evo and I climb in. Judith and takes the back seat with Sarah. The only thing that seems to be missing is the emerald necklace I hung off the rear-view mirror. I fire Rovy up but keep the lights off. We bounce over the coral road, our tires kicking up a haze of white powder. I race down the hill but slow for the divots. I hang a right when we reach the highway and switch on the lights. We cut through foothills. The road flattens. The dash lights Evo's face. Her eyes are fixed on the road and Super Shorty rests on her lap.

I reach under the front seat and pull out the holstered Beretta. I slip the holster on. It feels good having firepower. I glance in the rear-view mirror and see Judith with her arm around Sarah.

"You saved us, Judith," I say.

"You saved us too, Tony."

The land's dark except for the occasional flash of a campfire. A man in a green parka signals us to stop with a flare. I floor it. We pass splintered barricades and police cars. The road curves through redwoods. I brake for a yellow dog in the middle of the road.

"Stop," says Evo.

I pull over. The dog hobbles to the shoulder on three legs. Evo swings open her door and is out on the highway. "Here," she calls, "come, boy!"

The dog drops down on the shoulder and cries.

Evo jogs over. "Good, dog," she goes, "you're our Cosmo."

*   *   *

I drive PCH into the dark morning. Cosmo's safe inside—he's sprawled across Judith's lap and has his head resting on Sarah's knee. I like the sound of the tires churning the road. We reach the 101 at sunrise and meander through the lowlands. Most of the acres are fenced. Horses graze in the distance. Evo stirs. We pass a dairy farm missing its cows. I switch lanes to avoid a stalled motor home and follow a bus into Gilroy.

Judith finds a tear in Cosmo's paw. I pull over in a garlic field and dig out Dave's emergency kit. Evo leashes Cosmo and leads him into the field. Judith searches through the kit and pulls out cotton swabs, hydrogen peroxide, and sutures.

"Can you do this?" I ask her.

"Midwife basics," Judith replies.

"Mom's practically a doctor," brags Sarah.

We join Evo. She's sitting beside shoots of young garlic. Cosmo rests beside her.

"Can we sedate him?" Evo asks.

"No," says Judith. "Hold him, Tony."

Evo gives me the leash and I wrap it around my left hand. I sit beside Cosmo, flip him on his back, and clamp my legs around his sides. Evo holds his front paw while Judith cleans the wound. Cosmo squirms. Judith uses forceps to submerge a threaded needle through his paw. Cosmo yelps. Judith begins "a running suture." Cosmo kicks, but my legs are clamped tight. Judith continues. After a final run, she knots the thread and bandages the paw.

"Finished," says Judith.

I unclamp my legs and Cosmo gets up. He limps on his bandaged paw.

"Owe you one," I tell Judith.

"No," she answers, "I owe you."

STANFORD

THANKS TO THE GAS we scored from Ajax, plus my spare gallons, we make it to San Jose. A crop duster buzzes the 101. Abandoned cars and SUVs block the slow lanes. This city's a tangle of concrete overpasses, flyover ramps, and cloverleaf interchanges. A mushroom cloud blooms in the sky. I veer from the fast lane to avoid a burning RV. Birds hover, uncertain where to land. A pack of gulls circles the Knight-Ridder Building. Plywood-and-tire shacks line a concrete barricade. We enter a world of drifters, skinheads, and loose dogs. Tramps are huddled on freeway cement using newspapers and cardboard for blankets. A kid tilts a wheelchair and a man tumbles out. Beds, couches, and mattresses are everywhere, even on a rise above the freeway. Smoke from campfires feeds the burnt-gray sky. A Chihuahua leashed to a van's hood barks as we pass.

"Stop for gas?" Evo asks.

"Not in this pit," I tell her.

*   *   *

I take the San Antonio ramp and reach Palo Alto. Men chainsaw hunks of meat out of a dead cow on East Meadow. A basketball game at Cubberley High pits Asians against whites. I hang a right on Alma Street and scoot by tri-level complexes and shingled bungalows. The sun filters through the redwoods. I go left on Churchill, skirt the Paly field, and stop for an army of zombie-eyed refugees following the rails north. Most are middle age or older. They either tow luggage on wheels or are pushed in wheelchairs. I see soft bodies forced into hard times, their half steps filled with the defeat of losing everything.

"I lived here for a winter with George," Judith says from the backseat.

"Boyfriend?" I ask.

"Yes. The complete opposite of Abraham."

"How so?"

"George was an atheist. His only god was himself."

There's a break in the refugee flow so I creep over the rails. I take El Camino Real north. The red dome of Hoover Tower looms over a eucalyptus forest. Stanford's dirt fields have become a village of motor homes. Alums with school caps and shirts congregate beside a lunch wagon. Kids on the curb wolf hotdogs and gulp from plastic cups.

I pull into a strip mall and park between a police car and a truck. Vines grow on the brick storefront of Fat Albert's greasy spoon. I climb out and stretch. The restaurant's picture window is shattered and a pool of glass glistens on the brick walkway.

"We should walk Cosmo," Evo says.

"Let his paw rest," I tell her.

Judith and Sarah get out. Judith pulls off her snood—her hair is in a bun, held by pins. Sarah pulls the pins. Judith shakes out her blonde hair and it falls to her shoulders like a gold stream. Her face is covered with freckles. She looks like a hippie chick in her peasant top and white bellbottoms.

We venture through a mall littered with pill bottles, bullet casings, and syringes. Men crouch on sleeping bags under the canopy of Peet's Coffee & Tea. Teens snort powder off a compact through straws. I kick a pill bottle—it sails and nearly hits one of them. They ignore me.

The scorched campus of Palo Alto High is across Embarcadero. We all cross El Camino. Men in Stanford football helmets spread out on the other side. They've got golf clubs and bats. They look like fathers and grandfathers. One with a turkey neck uses his club like a cane. They close ranks when we reach the curb.

"When's kick-off?" I ask.

"Gotta comedian," goes Turkey Neck.

"Any gas to be had, gentlemen?"

A big man grimaces through his face guard. He taps the tip of his Louisville Slugger against his palm. "See Po," he tells me, "over at the church."

"Where's that?"

"In the Commons," says Judith.

"That little fuck!" Turkey Neck snarls.

I see a boy lugging a metal safe through a eucalyptus forest. He's trying to run but the safe's too heavy.

"That's our cornerstone box," says the big man. "After him!"

The helmets give chase. The boy zigzags through the white trunks and disappears behind a green utility truck.

Judith finds a path through the trees. We reach a sprawling pavilion of slate buildings, bubbling fountains, and sculptured hedges. Redwoods spring from sylvan gardens. Ivy crawls the façade of the Stanford Union up to its red-tiled roof. Antique gas lamps and giant vases festoon the library's courtyard. We enter an arched hallway, our steps reverberating off the Ionic columns. This campus feels holy, as if the angels and a legion of saints will appear to take up earthly residence. We arrive at a massive church with exterior murals, flying buttresses, and a Gothic spire. I jam my shoulder into a wooden door, and my posse enters. The church smells of frankincense. Stained glass panels form an upper band of color below the buttresses. A black-robed priest stands beside an altar filled with crystal bowls.

Judith takes the center aisle through the rows of pews. We follow her past a kneeling congregation with orange-bead chokers. The priest taps a crystal bowl with a gong. "Yum," goes the congregation. A woman and a man kneel on zabutons on either side of the altar. The woman blows bullfrog notes out of a didgeridoo while the man plucks the strings of a sitar.

"There he is," Judith says.

She leads us to a black man in the last row. He wears a yellow sarong. His eyes are shut so tight his lids are wrinkled. An Asian woman kneels beside him. The pew behind them is stacked with red cans. I smell gas.

"Greetings, Po," Judith begins.

His eyes remain closed. A jeweler's glass is attached to the chain around his wrist.

"Po?" goes Judith. "I'm Judith. The one from Fort Collins?"

The Asian woman nudges his shoulder.

Po cracks an eye. He seems perplexed focusing on Judith. The second eye cracks. "My word," he says, both eyes going wide. "Judith Marie Bailey, from my last class in the old world. What brings you to town?"

"I'm going north, Po. Can we buy gas?"

"Do you still believe, Judith?"

"Yes. I believe."

"Favorite teaching?"

"The Prodigal Son."

Po winks.

The Asian woman nudges him again. "Gahng yeh soh."

Po nods. "Pardon the interruption," he tells us. "Do you have gold or precious gemstones?"

"We've got silver," I reply.

"You bring a truckload?"

"Depends. How much per gallon?"

"Ten ounce," the woman answers.

"Six," I offer.

Po smiles. His teeth are as white as snow. "That works," he says, "but only because you're with Judith. Will you keep her safe?"

"Yes," I go, "Scout's honor."

HALF MOON BAY

WE TREK NORTH through Menlo Park, the former home of Facebook. Kids dodge traffic selling bottled water and ceramic Mother Marys. There was a rumor Mr. Z built a bunker on the Facebook campus after his psychic predicted nuclear war. He'd admitted to the *Palo Alto Weekly* his passion was storing blood in solar-powered coolers so he could make money after the fallout. I crush an OCCUPY MENLO sign. People dig through boxes of paperbacks on the steps of Kepler's Bookstore.

"Why the book craze?" Evo asks.

"Think about it," Judith replies. "No TV, no tablets, and no internet."

"Only books and board games for entertainment," I add.

The sun moves toward the ridge of Ranch State Park. We reach Redwood City, a highway town strung together with strip malls, car lots, and specialty shops selling everything from cigars to trophies to carpet remnants. Girls dance around a boom box next to a wig shop. Men in cars and trucks crawl by checking out the girls. Dusk makes me nervous, as if shifting to darkness brings bad karma.

Evo taps my arm. "Potty break time."

"Can't we wait?" I grouch.

"Cosmo's been holding it for hours. Besides, he needs water."

I park beside a hedge of red hibiscus.

"Back in a flash," Evo says, hopping onto the sidewalk. The cargo door opens and she leashes Cosmo.

"Should I go with?" I call.

"We'll go," volunteers Sarah.

"Excellent," I say.

Judith and Sarah join Evo and they take off down El Camino Real. Cosmo pulls hard against the leash despite his bandaged paw. They have to hot walk to keep up with him, at least until he lifts his leg over a bush.

I get out and study the sky. It's too early for stars but Venus glows in the east. I wonder about Portico. I think about Evo and me, how the life we knew is gone forever. Yet strangely, I feel more alive in this new world that I did in the burbs.

"You," comes a voice. "Star Gazer."

I turn.

The cargo door's open. A fat Asian kid with bleached cornrows cradles my Panther. He raises the black barrel. "Got grinds?"

"I'll ask you kindly to give that back," I tell him.

"Finders keepers."

"You didn't find it."

"Shut the fuck up and drop your drawers."

"Why?"

"I wanna see your surprise."

"I have no surprise."

He stares through the scope. "Well, you had this blaster, and that surprised me. Strip."

I unbuckle my belt. I wonder what part of me hangs in the crosshairs. I can't get shot with my own gun. I could pull the Beretta but a sudden move could end my life.

"Saw Lady Gaga," he boasts, "over at the beach."

"She hot?"

"Cold now," he says. "Oakland homie blew her away."

"What for?"

He quits staring through the scope, but the barrel's still pointing at me. "You hear that skank-ass sing?" he asks.

I unbutton my jeans and unzip the fly. I hope Evo's back in a flash. But I change my mind. I'd rather take a bullet than have us both killed. My forehead sweats. I pull the denim off my hips and drop the jeans to my knees. "You Chinese?" I stall.

"Pinoy."

"Is that Korean?"

"Filipino, dumb fuck. Drop your BVDs. I wanna spock your shriveled white marbles."

"You gay?"

"Shut the fuck up."

I hook my thumbs under the waistband of my Joe Boxers and slide them down over my hips. The Pinoy slants the barrel—I think he wants to crosshair my balls. Jesus, I think, I'm finito. I see Evo behind him reaching into cargo. She pulls out something metal with a handle.

The Pinoy taps the Panther's trigger. "Quit teasing," he tells me, "show those marbles."

A *wha-whoosh* echoes off the sidewalk, like the sound of a tire getting stabbed by a stiletto.

He drops my rifle and careens off, a hand fused to his neck. Blood spurts. "Motherfuckin' bitch," he goes, "fuck my ass raw!" He falls off the curb and stumbles along the gutter splashing a trail of blood. The girls keep dancing around the boom box as if nothing has happened. One turns up the volume.

Evo raises the nail gun. "Nailed him."

I yank up my boxers and jeans. "Where's Cosmo…and your escorts?"

"Ogling the wigs."

I pick up the Panther. The barrel's dented. Steel peeks through the black paint. I pull the bolt—a hollow point flies out and bounces off the sidewalk. The Pinoy didn't even need to load the chamber to blow me away.

Judith and Sarah return with Cosmo. I lift him in and we scramble back inside Rovy. My hands shake. Sweat beads up on my forehead. I fumble with the keys.

Judith pats my shoulder from behind. "You okay, Tony?"

"Sure," I lie. "Onward to Oregon, girls."

*   *   *

We take the 280 north and skirt the Santa Cruz Mountains. A blue Cuda zooms by. The driver taps the brakes but keeps hauling ass through the rolling hills.

"Was that?" I ask.

"Was that who?" goes Evo.

"Never mind," I tell her. My hands quiver on the wheel. We should stop for the night. The beach should be safe. Judith adjusts her reading light to illuminate the pages of The Bible. She wants

Sarah to read Revelation. Sarah says she's busy writing a poem in her journal. Judith insists that an understanding of scripture is the basis of all good poems. Sarah fights back—she tells her mother The Bible forces people to think and feel like sheep and that we should all strive to think and feel for ourselves. I grin. She sounds like any red-blooded American girl.

"Read your poem," I say.

Sarah groans. "It's not finished."

"What's it about?" Evo asks.

"Everything."

I take the 92 west. The gentle curves calm me. We cut through mountain passes and drift by patches glowing with pumpkins. I remember carving with Jimmy. As a toddler I thought, once you decided what you'd be your first Halloween, you always had to be that. I was Br'er Rabbit for three straight years before Dadio asked if I enjoyed "dressing like a silly bunny." Jimmy wasn't much help— he was always the devil.

*   *   *

Evo and Judith breaststroke through a bay shaped like a half-moon. Cosmo snoops the shore. The first stars are out. I find Venus. A band of pinkish light holds on in the west. The beach is wide and flanked by dunes. I walk the shore with Judith and we gather driftwood. She finds a stash of lumber below one of the dunes. I know she'll have a good life in Oregon, one far enough away from Malpaso to discourage Abraham from visiting. We return to our quilt spread over the sand. I stack my wood on a flat stone and Judith piles hers on top.

"Are you cooking, Tony?"

"No. But a fire makes things friendly."

I stick crumpled paper under a batch of kindling and light it with the FireSteel. A flame rises. Judith and I cozy down on the quilt. She admits Sarah is Abraham's daughter. I suspected as much, since she shares his midnight eyes, dark complexion, and thick eyebrows. Sarah turns thirteen on Christmas day. Judith runs her hand through her blonde hair. Her green eyes shine in the light. Her freckled nose makes her seem more like a Woodstock chick than a mother. She takes full blame for our imprisonment in the barn. She'd told Abraham she was leaving Malpaso with Sarah because of his abuse, not because of anything I said or did. I don't ask for details. She said we'd offered to take them with us to Oregon, and he threatened to poison them both.

"What about Evo?" I ask.

"He still wants First Woman."

"Will he come for her?"

"Yes."

"All the way to Crater Lake?"

"No. He'll go as far as the border and turn back. He's scared of the PA along Oregon's coast."

Judith says non-joiners are in unmarked graves alongside the coral road. The night we fled was perfectly timed—Abraham had split with Uriel for an emergency meeting in the Carolinas. Judith says he's starting a militia and plans on being the first U.S. President in the new world.

Evo and Judith swim in and Cosmo greets them. I pull out the 3-person tent. Judith helps me anchor the corners with steel spikes and watches me pound them in with a mallet.

"You had trouble in Redwood City," Judith says.

"Sure did. Good thing my better half's handy with nails."

I serve cold MREs, mostly because I'm too tired to drop a pot of water over the flames. Judith and Sarah take the tent. Evo makes a bed of sleeping bags for us beside the fire.

I gaze up at the sky, my arm around Evo. I can't find Polaris. The future feels strange, and I can only hope we'll find markers to lead us safely through California into Oregon. A comet streaks east to west and burns out thousands of miles away over the sea. I pray for Evo and our unborn child.

THE BORDER

AT DAYBREAK, I return to the 280 and hop on the 101. We zip by the cities of San Mateo, San Bruno, and Pacifica. I avoid the turnoff for South San Francisco because a cement mixer blocks the ramp. It's been smooth sailing, although I did have trouble weaving through a mob walking the freeway. We scoot by Candlestick Park. The hills are stacked with yellow, green, and pink box-shaped bungalows. We pass Russian Hill, a ritzy enclave of high rise condos and mansions perched on the water. Alcatraz is a shadow island offshore. The triangular tower of the Transamerica building pierces the fog. San Francisco seems strangely untouched. Districts are clustered with hotels, office buildings, subdivisions, and parks. The only smoke comes from Coit Tower. I can see the Ferry Building on the waterfront. A ferryboat's marooned in the bay and ships have run aground on the Embarcadero's shore. Oil tankers are parked three-deep along the piers. Market Street splits the city in half and cars move up and down the wide boulevard. Mount Tamalpais is a green mound behind San Francisco. Dave said a missile destroyed the Oakland Bay Bridge and that we should avoid Oakland anyway since the Hell's Angels are running drugs and prostitutes at the Wild Game Refuge in Lake Merritt. We make the tollbooths for the

Golden Gate and Rovy rumbles over the bridge's metal gratings. The ocean looks gray beyond the cables.

"Angel Island," says Judith.

I zigzag through outbound lanes blocked by abandoned vehicles. I'm forced into the inbound lanes to avoid a white-uniformed man standing beside a table stacked with crabs. "Dungeness," he calls, "bay scallops!" A woman empties an urn over the railing—wind catches the ashes and sends them up like smoke signals. The northern side of the bridge is shrouded in fog. The *poppity-pop* of small caliber fire makes pedestrians duck. I zip around an ice cream truck and race for the fog.

*   *   *

It's a blur of foothills and evergreens from Mill Valley to Santa Rosa. Locals squat on the steps of the Santa Rosa Bank. Judith wants to visit the Luther Burbank Gardens to check out the orchids. "Not today," I tell her. A WELCOME banner in Arcata is strung between utility poles. The central square is a hodgepodge of wooden structures. COURAGE and HOPE flyers are pasted to lampposts. A President McKinley statue looms over a mound of books, backpacks, and laptops.

"George," Judith says, "George Fargo!" She waves at a rail thin man near the square's fountain. He's got on overalls and a porkpie hat. He takes the final pull from a bottle and hurls it at us. The bottle bounces off Rovy's fender and shatters on the sidewalk. I floor it.

"Guess George didn't recognize me," Judith sighs.

"Guess not," I reply.

*   *   *

I weave through redwood forests and long stretches of beachfront. Indian summer has arrived. Judith and Sarah forage during out potty break stops. So far they've returned with wild mushrooms, raspberries, and edible flowers. The beaches are covered with campers and tents. I smell cooking. We pass Eureka and towns wedged up against the Redwood National Park: Azalea, Little River, and Trinidad. A school bus at Patrick's Point opens its door for thugs. The road becomes a checkerboard of light and shadow. Gulls perch in branches. We hit cold pockets of air. Drifters roam the highway. Most move in tribes and carry little more than backpacks or knapsacks. There's a zombieness to them, the same trudge I saw on Palm Springs Boulevard.

A tree blocks us in Orick. I go 4WD and climb over the trunk. A highway looping east would take us into the Siskiyou Mountains and get us to Oregon faster. But that road could be treacherous and Rovy hates hills. The gas we scored in Palo Alto will get us to the border. I decide to stick to the coast.

*   *   *

At dusk, I pull over beside a farmhouse in Crescent City. A skunk scurries through a pasture. I don't want to camp but we decide to rest. The reserve gas has already been tapped. Rovy hasn't been too happy with Po's fuel—she knocks on inclines and farts from her tailpipe. I curse myself for forgetting gas stabilizer.

I nod off, not aware of the time. I stir at four. I drive the dark morning to Oregon, with two sleeping women and a girl scribbling poems. We pass Crescent City and hop on the 199. The new highway cuts northeast through an ancient forest. Stars speckle a swatch of sky above the trees. We reach the WELCOME TO OREGON sign at dawn.

Evo celebrates by passing out strawberries. She cracks open a jar of carrot juice and fills four plastic cups. "To Oregon," she toasts.

"To our new home," says Judith.

BOOK 2

OREGON

K FALLS

WE SKIRT the base of Roxy Ann Mountain. I see rolling hills and snow on distant peaks. Golf courses frame Medford. Pines sprout from acres of dead shrubs and grass. I always thought everything was green in Oregon. We pass a pear orchard and take the Main Street ramp. Rovy farts past City Hall. Next is Carnegie Library, a building that reminds me of a Southern mansion with its columns, brick entrance, and sea of magnolias. A family picnics on the big green lawn. Medford's clogged with mobile home parks, retirement high rises, and ancient apartment complexes. Locals give us long hard stares. Edith's Pie Shop is open, but I don't like the looks of the guy out front sucking a corncob pipe.

"Cosmo needs a walk," Evo says.

I stop for a woman crossing. "Can it wait till the Rogue?"

"Push, push, push," she grouches.

I go north on Crater Lake Highway. The asphalt's silky smooth, and I like the hum of the tires. We pass country stores, strip malls, and shuttered cottages. I stop at a booth manned by a ranger in a brown uniform and a wide-brimmed hat.

I lower my window. "Good morning, Mister Ranger."

"Morning," he goes. "Road's out. You'll need to go through K Falls, if you want the crater."

"K Falls?" I ask.

"Klamath. Hit the 140 and head east."

"Are you the last?" Evo asks the ranger.

He hunches down, resting his forearms on the frame of my window. The crown of his hat is ringed with sweat. "Last what, miss?"

"Ranger. Are you the last Oregon ranger?"

"One of the last. On duty only because I thought good folks like you need guidance, to avoid what's coming."

"What is it?" I ask. "What's up the road?"

"Something deadly."

"How deadly?"

He grabs his brim. He tips his hat back, revealing a stitched wound running the width of his forehead. "Folks," he goes, "if you really want to know, it's where you meet your Maker."

* * *

We reach the Rogue River and speed east on the 140. The river churns through the gulch. Evo's edgy as hell. Her eyes are glued to the highway, and she's griping Super Shorty. The ranger said cops investigated a roadblock, but never returned. Medford vets from the Elks Lodge went up after them and they didn't come back either. A boy came out of the woods bloody—he said maniacs had blocked the road and were robbing everyone. Those who resisted got killed. Those who didn't resist were imprisoned in a locker beside the Rogue. The boy was cut by an ax while escaping, but not before he saw prisoners being led down the bank toward men with chainsaws.

* * *

Judith opens up about her life on the drive. She'd been married to an abusive man in Larimer, Colorado. He was a prison guard at Sterling Correctional, a Level 5 prison on the eastern plains, and he wouldn't allow her to leave the house because he swore she was seeing other men. Before Colorado shut Sterling down, Judith hopped a train bound for LA and hitched north. She worked with George Fargo at an organic store in Big Sur. Abraham, a frequent shopper, convinced them to sell everything and join Malpaso. I figured there wasn't much difference between the prison guard and Abraham. She said it was time to leave when Abraham wanted the PA as an ally. His trump card was a nuclear warhead stashed in the barn. He'd told Judith that, if the PA didn't give him Northern Cal, he'd turn Southern Cal into a wasteland.

* * *

We slip into Klamath. The homes are tiny and boarded up. A tortoise crawls the asphalt. White picket fences are everywhere. Garden gnomes guard the early pumpkins. An aquarium lies shattered in a driveway, its bright plastic plants glowing in a pool of shards. The door to a feed store is nailed over with irregular slabs of lumber. Men hang out on a curb passing a jug of wine. The rusted shell of a truck lies sunken in dirt.

Evo spots a white stallion tethered to a barbed wire fence. I stop and she frees him. The stallion trots past a group of teens and a boy pulls a gun. "Horse meat!" he laughs.

Our tires pop over gravel through a shantytown of shacks and derelicts. The road connects to a four-lane highway. We pass strip malls, gas stations, and used car lots. I veer to avoid a bulldozer tire blocking the lane. Next comes the Klamath Mortuary and Gibler's Health Foods. A man in a poncho wiggles a BABY FOR SALE sign.

"Stop!" says Judith.

"Scam," I tell her.

We reach a Circus Vargas tent that resembles a giant purple mushroom. Men sit on barrels drinking and smoking. Boys gather around a Mexican flag strung to a fence post. More boys hike down a hill toward them, their leader waving the U.S. flag.

"What's happening?" Sarah asks.

"Yashua will bring peace," Judith replies.

Whenever I hear "Yashua" I flash to Abraham. I look at Judith through the rear-view mirror. She looks worried, as if she was wrong leaving Malpaso. She sweeps blonde strands of hair out of her face.

Evo spots the sign for the 97 and I take it. We're two hours from the crater. We pass the KLAMATH NATIONAL WILDLIFE REFUGE sign.

"Break time," says Evo. "Back to that refuge."

"But we're so close," I argue.

"Nature calls, Tony. I'm sure our guests need a break too, don't you, girls?"

"Yes," they answer.

"Tony has a camel bladder," Evo says.

Sarah giggles. "Wish I did."

I do a 180 and head back. I pull off the 97 and take a skinny road into the refuge. The lake's to our right. We hit a strip of silky smooth asphalt, and I drive past willow-like trees drooping over the water. A mud flat offshore has a canoe stuck in it. Egrets and cranes graze the marshes. The open water pushes north—it's so wide that it feels like an ocean. I spot the silver bubble of an Airstream on the opposite bank. I shift to neutral and idle. I pull my binos from the door's compartment. The Airstream's surrounded by tents. A fire burns. A boy circles the fire swinging a net. A woman on crutches appears at the doorway and motions for the boy. I hear gunfire. Ducks flying low land on the mud flat.

"This feels weird," Sarah goes.

I put the binos back. "We're safe, Sarah. No worries."

I drive until the road ends and park in a lot heaped with garbage.

A tiny log cabin-style restroom sits on the edge of the lot. Ribbons of toilet paper hang off the pines around the cabin.

"Civilization," I say.

Evo swings open her door. "Walk Cosmo?"

"Sure thing."

They climb out and head for the cabin while I leash Cosmo. He's still bandaged because the sutures are still in. Judith changes his dressing every morning and wants to give it another week. Cosmo leads me into the refuge. His limp is gone. A green gate knocked off its hinges lies splintered on the path. We scoot around the gate and pass clumps of skunk cabbage. A raccoon claws up a fir. A bungee cord is stretched between birches, and clothespins cling to the cord. Cells and iPads hang off the branches on lines of catgut. The marshes are to my right. Oaks rise up on either side of the path, their branches forming a canopy above me. The sky looks like blue confetti through the branches and leaves.

"Hel-low," comes a voice.

Cosmo growls.

I face the marsh. A man with a red duck hunter cap struggles through the sedge in hip wader boots. His red beard matches the cap. He's got on a camouflage jacket and a wooden duck whistle hangs off a cord around his neck. He parts a patch of cattails.

Cosmo barks, tugging against the leash.

The man reaches the bank and holds up his hands. "White flag."

"Come on up," I say.

His boots make a sucking noise in the mud. He's favoring a leg and breathing heavy. He stinks of tobacco. He kicks the ground when he reaches us and mud flakes off his boots.

Cosmo snarls.

"Hey, boy," he says, holding out his hand.

Cosmo smells it and wags his tail.

The man pulls up his waders. "Don't mean to be un-neighborly," he goes, "but you'll find only heartache here. Malaria struck Upper Lake and two babies died yesterday. Head out soon, that's my advice."

Evo appears at my side. She's toting Super Shorty.

The man introduces himself as Brick. He tells us he's from Seal Beach, Oregon. The PA sent death squads, but Seal Beach militias banded together to battle the first wave. They shot a PA bigwig, but the PA countered with heavy artillery. The militias were defeated in a bloody battle that killed Brick's father and two brothers. He took a bullet in the thigh but managed to escape in the Airstream. Brick's eyes look hollow, as if he's seen too much. He warns of killers disguised as rangers. Evo asks if he has a wife and he says she's back at camp. They haven't eaten in days. "I'm lousy with a shotgun," he admits. He tells us the lake's fished clean and they're living on snails, lizards, and road kill. He's got four kids, including a baby. His sister split, taking the last of their supplies. "Ran outta shot," Brick says. "Spare a few cartridges?"

"Down to my last box," I tell him.

Cosmo sniffs his boots.

"Nice dog," he goes. Brick drops to his knees and presses his palms together like he's in Church. "Please," he begs, "if you could spare some food, anything, for me and my family."

"Off your knees," I tell him. "I've got MREs."

His eyes light up. "That would save us."

I lead the way back. Evo walks behind Brick. I see butterflies fluttering around a jasmine. We pass the log cabin and reach the lot. Judith and Sarah wait inside Rovy.

"Hello, ladies," Brick says.

Judith offers a half-smile. "Greetings."

I pass Judith the leash and she pulls Cosmo close. I pop the cargo door and grab an open MRE carton of stews and pastas. I find loose boxes of cakes and brownies and toss them in. I hand Brick the rations. "Dinner's on me," I say.

He hoists the carton onto his shoulder. "I thank you kind people for your generosity and wish you good speed. Heading north?"

"Yes," I go.

"Where north?"

"Washington," I lie. "Maybe Canada."

"Forget Canada. Canuck Army's got shoot-to-kill orders. Avoid the 62."

"How come?"

"Nasty tribes. They'll trap you on Rim Road and you'll never escape."

"What about Crater Lake?"

Brick shakes his head. "Wouldn't take my family there. They've got warrior tribes living around that lake and murderers at the lodge. Well, I thank you again." He hobbles off balancing the box. He takes the bank down and wades through the marshes. I grab the binos and spot children waiting on the opposite bank.

"Crater Lake's still a go?" Evo asks me.

"I'm not sure."

I lift Cosmo in through the cargo door. Evo and I return to our seats.

I speed north on the 97 while Sarah punches the keys of an iPad she found. Judith sees snow on Mount Shasta. We pass a yellow sign with a silhouette of a farmer on a tractor. The pastures are covered with dead cows. Barns melt on the plains, their rickety forms being absorbed by the red dirt. We reach the turnoff for Highway 62 and I crank the wheel. Jesus, I think, what if Brick's right about warriors and murderers? Damn. But we've come so far it would be foolish to head into Washington. Winter's not far off. I don't want to be like Brick: no food, no ammo, lousy shelter, and a family on the brink of starvation. We'd eat through the MREs in a month. I'd have to hunt. I'd have to kill for four every day, all with a baby coming. The ammo would vanish. And where would we live? All crowded inside a 3-person tent? If I die, I doubt they could make it on their own. We should be part of a tribe, where other men can pick up the slack if I fall.

Sarah lowers her window and tosses out the iPad—it *clackity-clacks* on the highway.

Evo taps my arm. "Penny for your thoughts."

"Stay positive," I tell her, "we'll find a good home."

CRATER LAKE

I HUG THE EDGES of a horseshoe driveway. The tires squeal. Birds pluck red berries off bushes. A four-floor chalet with stone walls beckons in the foreground. It has a green roof that angles like a tricorne hat and all the rooms have bay windows. I park beside a black Hummer.

"Judith," I say, "you and Sarah stay put."

"How come?" asks Sarah.

"I need to see who's in there."

"We'll wait," Judith promises.

I get out. Evo's already on the walkway stuffing shells into Super Shorty. I leash Cosmo and he tugs me to the stairs. I follow him up, pulling my Beretta. A *Do Not Disturb* sign hangs off the knob of the pine door. Evo waits halfway up the stairs.

"One in the chamber?" I ask her.

"Always."

My knock sounds weak so I bang with my fist.

"Forget to make reservations?" Evo asks.

"Hoping for a cancellation."

"Creepo at the window!" Sarah calls from Rovy.

"Gotta gun?" I go.

"No."

I turn the knob—the door cracks an inch.

Cosmo nudges open the door with his nose and tugs me inside. Evo's behind us. The lodge is dark, even after my eyes adjust. Curtains shroud the windows. The ceiling's high, with pine beams intersecting at 90 degrees. The wood smells good, a scent that reminds me of summer cottages. But this isn't a cottage. The walls are block lava, and the slats of the wooden floor creak with each step. There must be a hundred rooms.

Evo opens a curtain. "Let Cosmo go," she says.

I unleash him. He sniffs a bear rug in front of a fireplace. I smell hard liquor, burnt wood, and cooked meat. A vertical support column is stripped of paneling. Evo follows me over a Persian rug. A porcelain vase on a marble stand is stuffed with wilted violets. A cold breeze blows in through an open window and the dead flowers rattle.

"The Great Room?" asks Evo.

I tuck the Beretta back in my holster. "Yeah. Not so great now."

Evo opens more curtains. Leather couches line the lakeside wall. A map's tacked to a post: a hand-drawn canoe floats in Danger Bay and I notice a big red X running through Wizard Island. A table has a hatchet stuck in it. A tin beside the hatchet is stuffed with hooks, rolls of catgut, and golf balls. I pluck out a ball. "Here, boy," I say, "come, Cosmo." He ears twitch. I underhand the ball. It hits the ceiling, bounces off the hardwood floor, and rolls.

Cosmo bounds after it.

Evo snoops in the dining room while I check out the fireplace. The brick façade's black with grit. Ashes spill out of the pit. I hold my hands over the ashes—they're still warm. Cosmo drops the ball at my feet.

I toss the ball again but Cosmo ignores it.

Rustling comes from behind the lobby desk. I pick up a poker.

A man wearing a black beret appears. Gray hair spills out from beneath the beret down to his shoulders. "Welcome to the lodge," he goes. He's got a lantern jaw, bushy eyebrows, and a nose that looks like it's been flattened in a fight.

"Oh, Evo," I call.

She jogs the wooden floor and joins me. We approach a desk cluttered with maps, pens, and a pyramid of Spam cans.

"You it?" I ask him.

He clasps and unclasps his hands. "Yes," he replies. "Been on my lonesome for what seems like years."

"No tribe?"

"Tribe? You kidding? Only crazies live in places with zilch food, bad heating, and smothered in snow half the year. Fishermen came last week but didn't catch a thing. Water's clean though. Cleanest water you'll find."

"No fish?"

He eyeballs Evo. His face is smoothly shaven, except for patches under his nose and near the tip of jaw where he missed with the razor. I sense he wants to trust us yet is wary of our intentions, as if we have the power to evict him.

"Any trout?" Evo presses.

"Rainbows," he replies. "But I've seen Kokanee, Coho, even a few browns. You plan on spending the night?"

"Not here," I tell him. "We'll camp on Wizard Island."

"Privacy over there, but deadly cold."

"We've got thermal sleeping bags and a tent."

He smacks his face. "Watch for bugs. Mosquitoes big as bats, suck the life outta you."

"That your Hummer out front?" Evo asks.

"No, I'm a two cylinder man. That junker was anchored here the day I checked in. Tank's bone dry."

I hear scampering and turn—a mouse scurries over of the bear rug and disappears under a couch.

"Pocket mice," the man says. "Common in Crater Lake. Pack rats too, but they feed at night. One swiped my watch and another stole tea bags. Wish I had a cat."

"Gotta gun?" I ask.

"12-gauge, but only three shells."

"Any food?" Evo asks.

"You two sure ask a lot of questions. You lawyers?"

"Hardly," I chuckle.

"Canned food mostly," he answers. "Spam, stew, peaches. Pantry got raided. I found a secret stash of corned beef hash, kidney beans, and even Almond Roca."

"Still with us, Crater Man?" comes a static-filled voice from a room behind the desk.

"Ham radio?" I ask.

"Sure is. Fella's gotta have some entertainment now, don't he?"

"BHRO?"

"Crater Lake Outpost," he salutes, "at your service."

"You know Dave?"

"Dave who?"

"Dave Draco, from Pinyon Crest."

"No."

"Ran a ranch called Nirvana, near Palm Springs."

"You mean Mr. Nirvana, pioneer of the Mojave?"

"That was him."

"Was?"

I nod. "Dave was a good friend."

"Damn shame," he says, shaking his head. "Excuse my manners. Name's Percival."

"Knights of the Round Table," goes Evo.

"I'm Percival Peabody. But you can call me 'Percy.'"

"I'm Tony," I tell him, "and this is Evo, my better half."

"Just you two?"

"A mother and daughter rode up with us."

"You're all welcome," Percy says. He tips over a box loaded with empty Spam cans and starts building another pyramid on the desk. He tells us he's been at Crater Lake since April, after finding a Honda 215 stashed in a confessional at the Old North Church. "One if by land, two if by sea," he chanted as he puttered for the Continental Divide. He snuck into the lodge on April Fool's Day and hid in the cellar with the rats. "Got real strange," Percy says. There was disco dancing in the Great Room, doors slamming, windows shattering. Someone took an ax to the concierge desk and used it for firewood. Gunfire came from across the lake. A buck was strung up on a hemlock. Flares glowed over the lake like moons. The following morning he pulled out his spyglass and studied the lake through the cellar window. He spotted girls swimming near Phantom Ship Island. He lived on wine and Spam for months and almost never left the cellar until he noticed a canoe drifting over from Danger Bay. The canoe ran aground on the shoals of Wizard Island and he ventured over. The canoe was loaded with gold bullion, MREs, and a 12-gauge. A bonfire raged in Cloudcap Bay. Percy raised his spyglass and saw naked women dancing around the flames.

"They still dance?" I ask him.

"Who's dancing?"

"The naked women."

"Haven't seen a soul in months." He slides open a desk drawer and pulls out what looks like a red brick with an antenna. "Here," he goes, tossing it.

I snag it. "Walkie-talkie?" I ask.

Percy nods. "Stuffed that relic with lithium. We could gab for years, not that I'm a motor mouth or anything."

"Any organic food?" Evo asks.

"Gotta garden," Percy says. "Mostly zuchs and cherry tomatoes, but I'll have squash in September."

"Time for us to go," I tell him.

"Wizard Island?" he asks.

I smile. "We're island folk, Sir Percival."

WIZARD ISLAND

THE ISLAND IS A CINDER cone on the lake's western edge. It looks like a rabbit's head floating a velvety blue sea. Trees thrive on shore but thin out going up. A string of boulders in Skell Channel leads to the island. Stepping stones, I think. Fumarole Bay is on the island's western shore. North of the bay is Emerald Pool, a bright green rectangle of water cut in the lava.

Judith wants to stay at the lodge. Percy gave a tour and showed her and Sarah a pantry with canned food on its shelves. Now Judith has the key to a top floor suite, one with a lake view.

I'm not sure what's on Wizard Island. Part of me wants to pitch tent on its shore. Another part doesn't. We tug on our wetsuits, hiking boots, and head down with daypacks slung over our shoulders. I lead with my right foot and drag the left. Cosmo barks thinking I've invented a new game. Evo baby-steps it, her arms spread like wings.

The descent's treacherous. Each step kicks up volcanic dust. I disturb cinders and create mini cascades. Evo's steps are light and careful. We reach a hemlock-and-fir forest and I snatch at branches for balance. I steal glances at the lake through the needles and can't remember a blue so dark, one that turns indigo beyond the island. A chunk of lava breaks off—I fall and start to slide.

"Tony!" Evo calls.

I jam my left foot into the trunk of a Shasta fir and stop. Cosmo sticks his wet nose in my face. He's still got his paw bandaged.

Evo holds out her hand.

I take it and she pulls me up. "I'm a natural klutz," I tell her.

"Cosmo enjoyed it."

"Onward?"

"Sure. I wanna swim in that pool."

I continue my dragging technique and more dust swirls. Ponderosas mix with the hemlocks and firs halfway down. We ease through a gulley and the sharp descent becomes more gradual. Cosmo's already running the crater shore. Evo spots a sleeping owl.

We finally reach the shore and pull off our boots. Cosmo leaps into Skell Channel. He swims to the first stepping-stone offshore and climbs up. I tuck my boots into my pack and wade out. The water feels like ice even in a wetsuit.

I look back. "Jump in," I tell Evo, "the water's fine."

She sticks in a foot and winces.

"You'll get used to it, Babe."

Evo gets in. We wade a channel floor of stones and pebbles. Cosmo's bandage floats by. When the water reaches our waists, we hold the packs over our heads. We reach Cosmo's stone. Evo climbs up first and I follow.

I pat Cosmo. "Good boy!"

He shakes off water and barks.

We go stone to stone through Skell Channel until we reach the island. Emerald Pool is a brilliant green. Gray stones on the pool's bottom are streaked with reds and yellows. I stick my hand in—the water's warm. Evo wants to swim but I convince her to explore first. We peel off our wetsuits and put on our shorts, tees, and boots. I'm glad we brought boots because the ground is a mixture of cinders and wicked shards. Evo finds a level clearing halfway up, one with a lava ledge overlooking the lake. A belt of snow wraps around the crater shore. Egrets fly over the water and I follow their path back to Emerald Pool. I slip behind Evo and wrap my arms around her. "Was Dave right?" I ask, kissing her neck.

"Yes."

Our island does feel like a castle hewn out of lava, a fortress surrounded by a protective moat. Winter will be brutal but maybe we can build something. I pray that weather's our only worry until the baby's born.

*   *   *

At dusk that first day, Evo and I headed back to the lodge after Percy's walkie-talkie invite. The hike up was safer than going down.

203

Percy served everyone Spam, tomato salad, and fried zucchini in the dining room. I knew he was trying to make a good impression because he'd shaved off the hair under his nose and on his jaw, but there were nicks in his face where the razor had caught. Sarah loved the zucchini. Evo said the beefsteak tomatoes were "to die for." Judith avoided the Spam so I slipped her slices under the table to Cosmo. It got too dark to return to Wizard Island so Evo picked out a room next to Judith's.

*   *   *

At dawn, Percy showed us his path down, one that started at Lookout Point and wove through a narrow gulch. He lent us his canoe, and we floated supplies over to Wizard Island. Now I'm lugging our tent up to that clearing with the ledge. Evo lent me her fanny pack and that's where I keep the walkie-talkie. The air's clean and crisp. I reach the clearing and realize I left the steel spikes back in Rovy. I hatchet chunks of wood from a hemlock's trunk and shape pegs. I peg the tent's sides, using the hammer end of the hatchet to drive them through the volcanic soil. Evo arrives. She hangs our solar shower off a ponderosa and fills the shower's black bag with her canteen. I help her spread wool blankets inside the tent and unfurl sleeping bags over the wool. I consider it a good campsite, at least through summer.

*   *   *

At sunset, we sit on the ledge and watch ducks fly v-formations. Geese leave our bay for Phantom Ship, a smaller island southeast of us. The deep water turns to onyx. The lake seems to expand as twilight approaches, the shores moving farther away. I dig aluminum cups out of my pack and fill them with Evo's canteen. We'll never have to struggle finding clean water, as long as we stay. "A toast," I go, handing a cup to Evo, "to Oregon."

"To the god of the lake," she goes, raising her cup.

We clink and sip the best water on the planet.

*   *   *

The morning comes hot and bright. Doves coo drowsily from the trees. Evo's not in the tent. Neither is Cosmo. I pull on my trunks, duck under the flap, and hustle to the ledge. I stand before a blue circle of glass. White marks that look like crooked fingers streak the surface. "Evo," I call. "Evo?"

"Down here!"

I spot her in Emerald Pool. I jog down a path of cinders and cannonball in. The water's warm. I surface and grab the lava side. Evo swims over and wraps her legs around my waist. I let go. The streaked stones look cool below and I'm guessing it's ten feet deep. We float down until my feet touch bottom. I look up and see sky through the water and the bronze of Watchman's Peak. Evo's hair halos her face. I kick off the bottom and we rise.

Evo and I bake on stones. Cosmo joins us. I wonder what madness is going on in the new world. Percy says the borders between states are history and that militias battle gangs for control of the cities. The PA's pushed north to Canada. No word of the U.S. military. I worry about Evo and wish we had a doctor. I can only hope that Judith will pull us through.

*   *   *

We hike for the top after an MRE snack of cinnamon scones. A northern breeze cools us. I stumble across a campsite in a clump of Douglas firs. Red Bull cans, playing cards, and cigarettes cover a blanket. A circle of stones is filled with ashes. Half-burnt candles are fused to the stones. We find knives and forks, plates with the lodge's pine logo, and a Fossil wristwatch. A dartboard hangs off a fir, its bull's-eye filled with darts.

The cinders get smaller and smaller the higher we go. The firs and pines give way to hemlocks. Most of the hemlock branches facing north are dead. We reach the top of the cone and find a shallow dimple thirty yards across. Evo follows me into the dimple. A U.S. flag is tied to a ski pole that's tipped over. Evo rights the pole, wedging it deep. The flag flaps in the breeze. I imagine we're astronauts in the Sea of Tranquility claiming the moon with our astronaut dog. Evo finds a camouflage tent fixed with steel spikes. Maybe this was a scout's post, a tribe member keeping an eye on the lake. A black Mag-lite lies on a stump beside the tent. I pull out a leather courier bag from inside and unzip it. I find a quart of Jack Daniels, a box of .38 shells, and a *Sex Stories* paperback. I stuff everything back, zip up the bag, and toss it back inside the tent. "Let's keep moving," I tell Evo.

We continue through the dimple and up one side. My boots crunch the cinders. We climb out of the dimple and hike to the cone's eastern side. We stand beside a cluster of stunted hemlocks and gaze east at Danger Bay. Phantom Ship is below us, its reverse image playing on the water. Evo wants to enjoy the view so I leave her and trek along the edge of the cone. A crow, the first crow I've seen in Oregon, flies over me cawing. I find shell casings from high-powered rifles. Cosmo digs through cinders and I jog over. He unearths what looks like a soccer ball.

"What's that, boy?" I ask. "Whatcha find?"

What he found is not a ball at all—it's a skull. I shoo Cosmo away. A tuft of black hair clings to the crown and flesh hangs off the cheekbones.

"What is that?" asks Evo.

"A ball."

"That's no ball, Tony."

I grab the tuft and underhand the skull. It rolls over the cinders, sneaks between two hemlocks, and tumbles off the edge.

*   *   *

I set up the Coleman stove beside our tent at the campsite. I turn on the gas, light the burner, and plop on a pot of water.

The walkie-talkie crackles in the fanny pack. "Hello?"

"What's for dinner?" asks Percy.

"MREs," I tell him.

"No trout in the lake?"

"Not a single cast yet, Perc. How are your guests?"

"Busy harvesting. That Judith sure has energy."

"You like her?"

"Sure. Why not? Hey, Tony, you should start exercising that rod and reel."

"Patience, Sir Percival."

"Luck of the Irish," he goes.

"Roger out," I say.

Evo pops out of the tent. She hands me the rod and Dadio's old green tackle box.

"I'm lousy at this," I admit, inspecting a line missing its lure. But there are plenty in the tackle box. Dadio made sure to never run out of fishing supplies. Having his gear makes me feel more confident. "Tomorrow we'll eat fresh," I promise Evo, "tomorrow I serve trout."

She does the Warrior pose. "You're the man, Tone."

* * *

I hike Wizard Island in trunks and high-tops. White windflowers cover the beaches along the bays and inlets. I love how the blossoms open at dawn, turning the shoreline as white as snow. When I look out there's no lake bottom to see, only deep blue. I'm balancing the rod in one hand and the tackle box in the other. A wicker creel hangs off my shoulder. I told Evo I fish alone, so she's back at camp with Cosmo.

I find a path that leads to a tiny bay on the northern side. I put the tackle box down and stick the creel beside it. I thread line through the rod's guides. I flip open the tackle box and pluck out a goldfish-looking lure with a treble hook swinging off its belly. Another hook sprouts from the dorsal fin. I dig out a leader, pry open the snap, and secure it to the lure. "Bring me luck, Goldie," I mumble, tying the leader to the line. The boulders offshore are under a few inches of water. They're stepping stones like the ones in Skell Channel. I leap from shore to the first step. The water drowns my high-tops. I walk to its edge and leap to the next. My soles are lake level so it feels as though I'm standing on water. Cosmo whines from shore.

"Je-sus," I plead, "not now, boy."

He jumps in and paddles over.

I help him up and he soaks me shaking off water. "Evo!"

She peers over the ledge above me. "Catch something?"

"Call your son."

"Cosmo wants to be with you."

"He's scaring the trout."

"I thought fish were deaf."

"Trout can hear a pine needle drop."

"Here, boy," Evo claps, "come, Cosmo!"

Cosmo jumps in and swims back to shore. He sniffs the tackle box before disappearing around the tip of the bay.

I focus on the blue alley between the steps and the shore. I cast. Goldie plops in twenty feet away. "Blue Alley," I mutter, "rock my world." Goldie cuts low, and the treble hook catches bottom. I jerk the rod to free it and pick up the pace. I reel in and cast again. Goldie lands in a patch of windflowers. I have to twist the rod at an odd angle to plop Goldie back in the lake. I reel fast on my third cast, until Goldie's doing a water bug dance on the surface. Nothing rises. I cast a dozen times without a strike. I quit counting. My fluorescent lure looks like an alien fish. I cast for the far end of Blue Alley and reel nonchalantly, remembering my days fishing with Dadio and Jimmy. One summer Dadio chartered a fishing boat in Key West and Jimmy pulled in a marlin. The line jerks. My rod's suddenly alive, the fiberglass body warping so viciously that I'm sure it will shatter. A bully trout tears out of Blue Alley with Goldie lodged in its gill. It burns into the deep water, turquoise bubbles rolling off its silver sides. I pull hard to set the hook as my reel buzzes and line spins off the spool. I tighten the drag. The trout runs back toward Blue Alley. There's a violent tug and my rod quits warping. The line goes limp. I reel in. Goldie's gone. All that's left is the ball bearing barrel of the leader.

I hop from step to step and return to shore. I dig through the tackle box. A hook stabs me. "Goddamn," I growl, sucking my finger. The sun's hot on my back. My face sweats. It feels like the day's almost over and the sour taste of disgust burns in my belly. I spot a canoe. Percy and Judith are paddling for Watchman Peak.

"Any luck?" Evo calls.

I look up. She's on the ledge wearing her green bikini. I'm tempted to run up and hop in the tent, but I can't let her be a distraction. I wave meekly and continue digging.

"Tone?"

I keep my head down. "No luck yet," I answer.

I snip off the ball bearing barrel and examine a tangled ball of lures, feathers, buzzbaits, and spinners. I untangle a plump version of Goldie, one with a fatter tail and buggier eyes. "Greetings, Goldie 2," I say, attaching it to a new leader. I return to the step and spit on Goldie 2 for luck. I aim and cast. Goldie 2 lands on the last step. I jerk the rod and my lure plunks into Blue Alley. I imagine a pan on the Coleman, with floured fillets crackling in butter. "Eat 'em when you catch 'em," Dadio always said. I flick with an upward motion, giving Goldie 2 height and medium distance. I cast until the pines become silhouettes. I'm getting better at placing Goldie 2. I imagine I've got one minute left in the fourth quarter and need to heave a Hail Mary. "C'mon, Mister Trout," I beg.

"Tony?" Evo goes.

"Ten minutes," I answer, casting again. This time Goldie 2 sails over Blue Alley and lands in a pine. It's stuck. "Tomorrow," I grumble, "tomorrow's a new day."

CASTING FOR LUCK

I TRY THE ISLAND'S east end, casting into the morning water. Goldie 2 breaks the surface. I jerk the rod to make it appear as if my lure's a struggling fish and an easy target. The shallows are great for trout because insect eggs hatch in the warmer water. Percy said the lake is over a thousand feet deep. I get the feeling creatures live in the depths. I imagine fanged mouths watching from below, waiting for me to venture out so they can swallow me whole. I notice Evo strolling the shoreline with Cosmo. The beef stew MRE last night wasn't bad, so I'm not pressuring myself today. If I catch, I catch. Evo said the cheese tortellini was creamy and tasted like Nucci's back home in Vista.

I reach Governor's Bay on the south shore, where a meadow of purple flowers starting at the whitebark pines spills over a lava path down to the water. Percy says deer swim Skell Channel to eat the Wizard Island flowers. I continue on to Fumarole Bay and cast the width, alternating reeling speed between slow and fast. Are the fish scared of Goldie 2? Should I try a feather? Jimmy would. I check out the snow on the shore beneath Watchman Peak. White islands float on the lake, but they're really the reflections of clouds. A golden squirrel drinks at the shore. The rod suddenly whips down, the reel spinning out line. A pink fish with a huge head leaps. Salmon, I think. Percy says they're rare, but they're not rare now. He hits the water hard on re-entry, his pink body easy to follow. I let him run without tightening the drag. He knives through the blue trying to throw Goldie 2. "That's it, boy," I whisper, "easy now. Easy does it." I reel slow but steady. I can outlast him. "Come to Daddy," I coax, "that's it, boy." My biceps ache. I get him near shore but he makes another run, taking more line. He leaps again. The rod bends violently. I shift the angle so the line stays taut, but without too much drag. I reel him to shore. He's pink from his top down to his belly. Goldie 2's stuck in his gill. My left eye twitches. I guide him close and lower the net. I pull up—my first fish squirms in the netting. I carry him over to the creel. I'm too excited to tell to Evo. I want to keep fishing.

I get three more strikes and land a pair of rainbows. Both trout fought like champs, although nothing like the salmon. I'll feed everyone tonight. I feel good returning to camp. I flip open the creel for Evo.

"The Fisher King," she smiles.

My walkie-talkie crackles. "Hey, Sir Percival," I answer.

"Any fins?" he asks.

"Fish fry at sunset."

"About the hell time," he chuckles.

*   *   *

Fillets sauté in my jumbo fry pan. I've got the small pan over a second burner and I'm blending a sauce of butter, cream, and saffron. The aroma makes my belly rumble. Percy canoed over special ingredients, along with syrah from the cellar and cognac from the bar. I stir with a wooden spoon. The sauce is orange from the liquid saffron. I don't want it too hot because heat could curdle the cream.

Percy passes me a tin cup of cognac. "The hunter preparing his kill," he says, checking out the jumbo pan. "You caught Coho."

I sip cognac, the liquor stinging my lips. "How can you tell?"

"Thickness," he goes. "Cohos look like whales."

I scoot the fillets to one side and drop in two trout. They bubble and brown in the butter.

"The women have abandoned us," Percy says.

I see Evo leading Judith and Sarah along a cinder path above our camp. She's taking them topside, where they'll have a panoramic view all the way east to Grotto Cove. The clouds hugging the rim are streaked red. I flip the trout, turn off the gas, and drop a lid over the pan. Dinner will finish cooking as the sauce soaks in.

Percy circles the camp. The solar shower amuses him, especially since he's got hot water over at the lodge thanks to a propane generator. He slips into the tent. "Roomy," he goes.

"3-person," I tell him.

"Enough for a couple and their mutt."

"Hey, Percy," I say, "are we safe on Wizard Island?"

He eases out of the tent. "Safe from the weather, or safe from outsiders?"

"Outsiders."

He wanders over to the ledge and stares at the lake. The early stars glimmer. Geese fly over, wings moving through galaxies. "Safer here than the lodge," Percy tells me. "They'll come to the lodge first for shelter and food, the way you did."

"Nobody's coming, Perc."

He clears his throat. "Outsiders always come, Tony. No way to stop it."

Evo leads her explorers back and they join us at a crude table I hatcheted from a log of white pine. We sit on chairs canoed over from the lodge and have a great view of the western shore. Deer graze at Lookout Point. Percy pours syrah into four wine glasses. I sip wine as Venus crests the rim. Sarah samples a vegan smoothie she made at the lodge. Both Sarah and Judith wear floral headbands made of pioneer violets.

Percy plops his propane lantern on the table and fires it up. It's bright at first but he dims the light, until it feels like a restaurant. I return to the stove and lift the lid. The scent of saffron mixes with the aroma of garlic. I sprinkle on chives. I scoop the fish into bowls of angel hair pasta and ladle the sauce. Sarah spoons sautéed carrots, bok choy, and mushrooms onto salad plates. Evo carries the bowls to the table.

"This beats Malpaso," says Sarah.

We join hands as Judith says grace. She doesn't mention Yashua or even God and thanks the universe for good friends, healthy days, and tonight on this lake. We dig in. The saffron gives the fish a honey-like taste, and the angel hair has soaked up the sauce. The fish is the best I've had. The veggie medley is excellent. Nobody talks—we're too busy eating. The bowls are empty before I know it and Percy has a second helping.

Something wet tickles my elbow—it's Cosmo's nose.

Percy pulls a bone out of his bag. "Been waiting for the right moment," he goes, tossing it.

Cosmo snags the bone in mid-air and trots off.

Dessert is strawberry pie, compliments of Judith. Evo and Judith talk veggies and fruit, including how to blend the perfect smoothie. Percy tells us he doesn't use apple juice to sweeten his drinks and confesses to slipping in pulverized beets. He says he's got an antique juicer that he'll take it out of storage. Judith mentions the benefits of wheat grass and bean sprouts. Sarah excuses herself from the table to go play with Cosmo.

Percy looks at Evo. "When's your due date?"

"Winter Solstice."

"Starts getting cold in late October. Best to move over to the lodge."

"Cold at the lodge too," I say.

"You guys need stone walls, Tony. This snow's like nothing you've ever seen. It comes fast and hard and you'll die of exposure."

I pour more cognac. "Can we build something, Perc?"

"Like what?"

"An igloo," Evo jokes.

"Do the birds stay for winter?" Judith asks.

"Sure," Percy says. "You'll see snow geese and tundra swans at Christmas. We're not built for the cold like them."

I polish off the liquor. We talk about hopes and dreams as a three-quarter moon breaks over the rim. Percy's obsessed with canning. He's got all the equipment set up in his pantry, but needs help preparing syrups to keep the fruit preserved. Judith volunteers to help. He says he's got enough peaches and pears for two hundred cans. I ask Judith about her dreams, and she says she wants to start a midwife service. Percy says Judith could help a lot of women and girls, but that the snow seals us off. Evo says she's worried about a safe delivery. Judith promises her that she'll be fine.

A huge moth circles the lantern. A smaller one bangs against the lantern's hood.

"Getting late," Percy tells Judith.

"Can you make it for dinner tomorrow?" Judith asks us.

"Sure," says Evo.

"Vegan?" I ask.

"Eggplant parmigiano. Sarah's making yogurt salad."

"I'll bring fish," I say, "if I get lucky."

Percy gets up and stretches. "The luck's with you, Tony." He turns up the propane flame and heads down with Judith. She's having trouble on the cinders so he holds out his arm. Sarah jogs the cinder path from the cone.

"Hey, girl," I call, "you'll miss your ride."

"I'll catch up," she says. "Thanks for everything!" She runs with Cosmo at her side.

Judith's at the bow holding the lantern. Percy sits at the stern. Sarah reaches the canoe and climbs in. Cosmo barks on shore. "Go home, champ," Sarah says, "we'll play tomorrow."

Percy paddles off. We watch until the canoe makes it safely across.

I put my arms around Evo and pull her close. Her lips taste like saffron. We've come so far together, and I never want to lose her. Everything feels right with the world as the stars spin above us.

LAKE LIFE

EVO SLIPS ON her wetsuit every morning and swims Skell Channel to the crater shore. She hikes to the lodge and helps in the garden while I fish. Evo's a farmer. She discovered wild basil and now the lodge's pantry is filled with jars of fresh pesto. We all do sunset dinner over at the lodge or on the island. I've learned how to prepare fish in different ways: broiled, baked, stewed, barbecued, and of course pan-fried. Judith's a sauce expert—she's perfected a lemon-cream-and-dill sauce for the trout and also makes a great pinyon nut dressing for our kale, mint, and watercress salads. When I catch salmon, Sarah borrows Percy's bamboo roller to make rosemary salmon sushi. Percy wants to hunt but the women have discouraged him from killing on land. Shooting deer is a sin. He cooks tons of beans and garnishes his bean bowls with sliced Spam. I've resisted opening the MREs because they'll save us when winter hits. We still have kibble for Cosmo. I'm not worried about the day our kibble runs out—Cosmo likes fish just fine, especially heads fried in butter.

* * *

Salmon favor Fumarole Bay. Rainbow trout and browns hang

out in Blue Alley. Between these two spots I usually catch four or five fish by noon. Goldie 2 looks like a war vet with deep bites to her head and body. I tried a few feathers to give her a break but the fish prefer her orange glow and wobbly motion.

*   *   *

The night sky is our silver screen. Evo unfurls our quilt and we lie facing the Heavens. The stars, planets, and moon are our pals. Shooting stars are passing acquaintances. Polaris sets above Watchman Peak. Venus has been breaking over the crater at dusk and rising to meet Cassiopeia. Mars gets lodged in Orion's Belt. The crater makes it appear as if our galaxy is held in a chalice. We hear owls growling in the hemlocks and the mournful cries of deer. Sometimes we hear birds landing on the lake, usually the new arrivals that are too exhausted to do much more than float on water reflecting the light of a billion stars. Evo and I enjoy inventing constellations for our own private zodiac.

"Voici the Mongoose," Evo says.

"Where?" I ask.

"Northwest, just above the crater."

"Are those three stars on top his head?"

"Tail."

"Southeast," I say, "check out the Great Turtle."

"That's no turtle."

"No?"

"No way."

"So, what it is?"

"A jellyfish."

Cosmo usually camps between us. After the zodiac game I pretend I'm Captain Kirk of the Starship Enterprise and that we're on a mission to save our planet.

"If you're Kirk," Evo goes, "who am I?"

"Uhura."

"I don't look like Uhura."

"Princess Leia?"

"That's a different movie."

"I know. But they'd have hit it off, if they'd met."

"Not with Hans Solo handy," Evo claims.

The walkie-talkie crackles. I pluck it out of the fanny pack. "Am I interrupting an intimate moment?" Percy asks.

I press the Talk button. "We're discussing movie sex, Perc."

"Oh. Well, no biggie, but Judith's sure the pinyon nuts are stale. Evo, should she chuck 'em?"

"Save them for the martens," Evo replies.

"Good advice. Well, goodnight you two."

"Goodnight, Perc," we say.

*   *   *

The lake's level continues to drop. The high water stain ringing the crater walls gets higher and higher. The Blue Alley boulders are now a foot above water, their blond heads basking in the sun. I've stocked Emerald Pool with baby trout too small to eat and the pool's surface boils when I toss in grasshoppers. I won't have to fish this winter if those trout survive.

*   *   *

I rock in the hammock watching a naked Evo hop under the solar shower. What a bod—she's got the hourglass shape of a *Playboy* centerfold. She tugs the cord. Water sprinkles out of the black bag above her.

"Warm?" I ask.

Steam rises off her skin. She plucks a towel off a branch and sweeps it over her skin. "Hot's more like it," she smiles.

"Stay naked."

"Yes?"

"Guinevere has been summoned by her favorite knight. Make haste into yonder tent."

"Your wish is my command, Sir Lancelot."

We duck inside while Cosmo naps under the hammock.

Evo sprawls out on the wool blankets. "Hey," she goes, "not fair."

"What's not fair?"

"Lancelot gets naked too."

I rip off my trunks and toss my high-tops. Evo is perfection, her tan lines are sexy and her skin reddish-brown. The baby bump's there but somehow that makes her more appealing in a goddess sort of way, as if she's linked to the lake and some higher force in the universe.

"Penny for your thoughts," she says.

I massage her feet and work my way up. Her skin's like silk. I could rub her all day.

The walkie-talkie sputters in my fanny pack. I fish it out and frown. I don't want to be a slave to the walkie-talkie the way I was with my cell.

"Hey, Tony," goes Percy, "you there? Hello?"

"That guy's got the worst timing," I tell Evo.

She laughs. "He's got sex radar."

"Emergency," Percy continues. "Red flag."

I press the Talk button. "What's the emergency, Perc?"

"Sort of."

"What's that mean?"

"We got company."

THE SNYDERS

THE SNYDERS ROLLED UP to the lodge in a yellow VW van screeching "Me and Bobby McGee" over tinny speakers. They had an outrigger canoe strapped to their roof and were towing a beat-up U-Haul trailer twice the width of their van. Steve Snyder was a refugee from the Czech Republic. His wife Kerstie was born in Sweden. Jacob, their thirteen-year-old, has his father's blond hair. They'd adopted a pair of cats Kerstie found on the road. Their story was unforgettable: they'd fled a castle town in South Bohemia and managed to get to Genoa where they caught the last ship crossing the Atlantic. But that ship was really a slaver bound for the Caribbean. As luck would have it, a rival New York ship faced off against the slave ship captain and sunk the slaver outside New York Harbor. A rescue boat took the Snyders to shore.

The VW van was filled with canned ham, eggs, and boxed artichokes. There were European delicacies in the trailer, such as smoked herring, Austrian chocolate bars, and Danish Puck cream. At first, I wanted them to leave. So did Percy. But the Snyders grew on us. They were helpful and friendly and became part of our Crater Lake family in no time. They fell in love with the lodge. Percy gave them a room on the second floor, one with a great view of the southern rim and Phantom Ship Island. Evo liked them so much she wanted to move to the lodge permanently. But, in the end, we remained on Wizard Island.

Steve gave me two yurts. He said he had no use for them at the lodge. Percy helped me and Steve set up one beside our tent and the second near the top of the Wizard Island cone. We call them Lower Yurt and Upper Yurt. It wasn't easy. We sledgehammered steel foundation spikes, attached bungee cords, and anchored the lattice walls after pegging them together. We raised slotted center rings for the rafter beams. After the rings and beams were secure, Steve helped me wrap the sides in canvas and slip on polyurethane top covers. The final step was adjusting the outer tension belts. A rafter beam splintered in Lower Yurt so Steve shaped a new one out of hemlock. Lower Yurt is forest green. Upper Yurt is terra cotta. The yurts give the island an exotic feel, as if we're not in Oregon at all but somewhere in Mongolia.

Lower Yurt is home. It's different living in a round space with a fire pit in the middle. We padded the cinder floor with yoga mats and spread out the wool blankets. Steve gave us his propane heater because the smoke from the pit was too much. Kerstie donated a rack. We have wine parties every Friday on Wizard Island, thanks to Percy's stash of Left Coast Pinot Noir and Del Rio Syrah. Judith makes honey-and-cream soda and other soft drinks for the kids, and she's perfecting a strawberry soda to be bottled using recyclables. Lower Yurt has indoor battery-powered lights. Wood crates serve as end tables. Our front yard and the path up from Emerald Pool are lined with a masterpiece of solar lanterns, compliments of Steve. He even helped lug up the rest of the gear in Rovy. The Beretta's wedged between two rocks in Upper Yurt. I keep the Panther and Super Shorty tucked in a Lower Yurt lava crevice.

Now we've got plenty of shelter on Wizard Island for guests wanting to spend the night—and they do. Whenever the Snyders sleep over, I cook scrambled eggs and buttermilk biscuits for breakfast.

*   *   *

Steve and Kerstie love Phantom Ship. They paddle around it for exercise and anchor along its shores. Kerstie braves hikes up the stone sails to pick glacier lilies, gooseberries, and mushrooms. She spotted a family of chipmunks living in one of the sails and brings them cashews from her nut stash.

"Did you see Alvin?" I ask.

"Yes," Kerstie replies, "and Theodore was there with the Chipettes."

Evo and Kerstie have become best buddies. They're both brunettes and could pass for sisters. They trek into the old growth forest behind the lodge and discuss Scandinavia nonstop. I'm glad Evo has Kerstie.

*   *   *

I play football with Jacob whenever I hike up to the lodge. Today, he's return man for the Phantom Ship Pirates. I'm defense for the Wizard Island Trout. I set the ball on a tee on the lawn between

Lookout Point and the lodge. Percy watches from the lodge garden with Cosmo.

"One play," Jacob calls, "all the way."

"We'll see about that, Bluebeard."

He jumps up and down. "Pirates rule!"

I kick off. Cosmo charges out of the garden. He beats Jacob to the ball and rolls it over the lawn with his snout.

"Interference!" goes Jacob. "Kick over."

"You don't know?" I ask.

"Know what, Uncle Tony?"

"The Trout just signed Cosmo. He's our free agent."

*　　　*　　　*

Percy slices apricots in half and tells me about the Chief of Crater Lake, the one who was killed in his sleep by a jealous lover. The chief's spirit still haunts the lake. Percy quarters the halves. "Turkish apricots," he tells me. Percy plans to fill thirty jars with dried apricots so we've got plenty for winter. He says to never "low ball" how much people can eat. He learned to stockpile in Boston when the grub barges quit running and the New Poor ransacked Harvard and BU for food. "Had to eat my shoes," he confesses.

"Percy," I go, "I've gotta to admit something too."

He looks up from his slicing. "If it's bad news I don't wanna

228

hear it."

"Dangerous is more accurate."

"I'm all ears."

I talk about Dave and Nirvana. I tell him how Dave got shot, about going gladiator, and how Royce's last words were, "Joe's a-comin'." I say Joe might be making his way north to track me down.

Percy's forehead crinkles. He quits slicing, flips open a cupboard, and pulls out a 12-gauge. The length of its double barrels surprises me. It's a solid shotgun. "You and Evo are my family now," he goes, "and Joe's dead meat if he shows."

"You don't have to do this, Perc."

He raises his hand. "Swear me in, Sheriff."

*   *   *

The canning goes smoothly. Judith and Sarah have perfected a special honey sauce for the peaches and pears. Percy boils the fruit before he transfers his bounty to a cold-water bath. That makes peeling easy. He slices the fruit for Sarah and she places the slices in mason jars. Judith drenches them in honey syrup. Percy seals the jars with sterilized lids and drops them in boiling water for twenty minutes. Next comes packing. Evo anchors the production line by stacking the jars in wooden crates. Percy wants some fruit dried so he's not canning apricots. We have fifty jars packed so far.

Sometimes Jacob visits to flirt with Sarah. He calls her "Peach Girl." He never stays long enough to help with the canning. Jacob claims he has more important things to do, such as chopping wood, fishing, and exploring Phantom Ship. Right now he's skateboarding the lodge walkway. Once he skateboarded the Great Room but Kerstie put an end to that. He pulled in a big rainbow trout yesterday, one he hooked in the channel between Phantom Ship and the crater shore.

Phantom Ship is mysterious and spooky. Steve was fishing offshore when something big took his line and cracked his rod. That keeps him going back. Strange how Llao's Fingers seem to swirl in the water off Phantom Ship, as if the slain chief is holding onto that island from the spirit world.

FISHING BUDDIES

STEVE AND I are fishing buddies. We leave the women behind and go adventuring. Steve's the better fisherman, especially when it comes to salmon. They're crazy for Loony Spoon, his green wiggle lure with the red eye. He's also more accurate with his casting. Truth be told, Steve's an artist blessed with luck. He's a master of the sidearm and the flip. He even uses the exotic shooter cast—he holds Loony Spoon's hook, pulls back until the rod bends, and bullets Loony out. I've caught more than Steve only once, but his three salmon easily outweighed my five trout. He wants me to switch to a spoon but I'm sold on Goldie 2.

We head to Phantom Ship in the outrigger and stroke with the wide Polynesian paddles. Waves *slap-slap-slap* against the keel. The island's reverse image plays on the water, its rock formations rising like sails of a ship. Hemlock, pine, and ponderosa cling to the jagged shore. I hiked it only once but didn't want to tackle stone sails rising 90 degrees vertical.

Our bow nudges the shore of an alcove. Steve tethers the anchor rope to a ponderosa. I ease out and wade over the submerged stones with the creel. We both wear trunks, tank tops, and sunglasses. I've

231

got on my San Diego Padres cap. Steve's wearing his lucky green fedora, the one he had on when he met Kerstie in Munich before Germany collapsed. I'm in high-tops and he's got on canvas shoes with rubber soles called "tabbies."

I put the creel down and we cast the shoals. My aim's erratic, as if I'm fishing for the first time. Stone frags lie below the surface, chunks that shattered off the sails. A midge fly buzzes my face. I swat it away. Last week, Steve tried a lure shaped like a midge but caught nada. No lure or feather works for him as good as Loony.

I get the first strike. My rod snaps down but snaps back when the tension slacks. I pull in a baby trout and release it. Steve casts in the shadow off a stone sail and gets the second strike. His rod bends viciously as he works the fish. A salmon leaps, it's body glistening and head shaking, trying to throw Loony. A log floats offshore and the fish heads for it. Steve tightens his drag. The salmon's dorsal fin slices the surface to ribbons as Steve guides it away from the log into the green water above a frag. He pulls hard and his rod looks ready to snap. The fish makes another run but tires in the shoals. Steve wades out. He reels fast and steady, until the fight is over. He drops his net and pulls up his prize.

"You're the man," I call over.

"Thanks." Steve drops the salmon in the creel. He returns to his spot and sidearms Loony Spoon. "Hey," he goes, "I think Percy and Judith are an item."

"Canning brought them together," I kid.

232

"She's too Biblical for him."

I cast out. "Perc can adjust." I look over at the crater shore and see a gorge of pines rising up to the rim that's easily the greenest spot on the lake. Snow clings to the walls of the gorge. It'll be tough fishing when snow pelts the lake.

I catch a rainbow and a second. Steve hooks a brown. We've caught enough for two nights, that is, if Percy and Jacob decide to make bean bowls and Spam their main course. Jacob lives for his next Spam fix.

"Reinforcements," Steve says.

The canoe coasts into the alcove. It's Jacob. His chest is golden brown from the sun and he's a strong paddler. He moors beside the outrigger. He's wearing my old RBV Longhorns trunks.

"What's up, son?" Steve asks.

"Wanted to see how you guys were doing." He puts down the paddle and wades in.

Steve heads beyond the point and casts into the deep water.

Jacob picks up a stone and skims it. He has Kerstie's blue eyes. He's the kind of boy that makes you ache for children of your own. But I worry he may be too kind and gentle for this new world. Could he defend us or even himself? You never know how someone will react until challenged. Outsiders will come. Some will be friendly. Others will want what we have and may be willing to kill for it.

Jacob wades back to the canoe and returns with a knife. He

hurls it and the blade bounces off a sugar pine. He retrieves the knife and throws a second time. It bounces again.

I put my rod down. "Can I try?"

"Sure, Uncle Tony."

He hands it to me. I grip the super light blade, one with overlapping leather strips for a handle. I flash to throwing knives with Jimmy. I flick the knife and it *thwanks* into the pine's trunk.

"Whoa," says Jacob. "What's the secret?"

"Pretend you're chopping wood over a fence."

"Huh?"

"Get the knife."

He brings it back. I show him how to hold the tip of the blade, bring the knife head-high, and release straight down.

He tries again but it bounces off.

"Don't flick," I tell him. "Flicking's no good."

After five more tries Jacob sticks it. "Hey, Uncle Tony," he goes, "can you teach me to shoot?"

"You mean, the Beretta I gave your Dad?"

He nods.

I'm not sure Steve would approve of me showing his son how to live-fire. But every kid should know the basics. I agree to teach him.

Steve rounds the point. He casts into the water beside the canoe.

"Wanna go jumping?" Jacob asks.

"Sure," I say.

"The fish are on vacation," Steve tells us, "so, jumping sounds like a plan." He places his rod beside the creel and rips off his tank. I take mine off too. I have no guilt having fun when we've already caught dinner.

Jacob heads to the outer tip and we trail behind him. I scoot around a cluster of ferns and see frogs clinging to a lodgepole pine. Jacob reaches a knoll we call the Jumping Off Place. Percy told me this is where souls jump from this world into the next. There's a 50-foot drop into deep blue and, if you look closely, you can see long strands of moss waving on an underwater frag.

Steve pulls off his fedora, sunglasses, and tabbies and walks to the edge. He raises his arms and shakes his legs.

"Swan dive?" I suggest.

He leaps, flying through the air headfirst with arms outstretched. He hits the blue hard, his legs wind milling. He surfaces. "What's my score, guys?"

"Nine," says Jacob.

"Four," I tell him, "and that's way generous." I hand Jacob my cap and sunglasses and walk over warm lava to the edge. We're on the easternmost edge of Chaski Bay. Danger Bay is due east and Eagle Cove's to the west. Wizard Island looks like an impossible swim.

"Jump, hotshot," Steve calls from below.

"Go, Uncle Tony!"

I hang my toes over the edge. It reminds me of diving at the Cove in La Jolla. I cannonball off and hit the blue, sinking deep enough to touch the stone sail with a foot. I brush away a strand of moss and kick through the icy water toward the surface.

My blood feels young.

THE HANGED MAN

I'M ON THE LEDGE near Lower Yurt on a misty morning. Droplets form on pine needles. The lake's gray from the clouds. Steve and I have plans to paddle over to Cleetwood Cove today, after Percy suggested we pirate the solar panels on the restrooms. We can use those at Lower Yurt. But, with weather like this, all I want to do is stay indoors with Evo. She's sprawled on our quilt in the yurt crocheting a bikini. Judith gave her lessons and yarn, and now she's hooked. Kerstie's birthday is next week and I know what she's getting. I told Evo I won't wear anything knitted, except a sweater, and to forget about crocheting me boxers or trunks.

*   *   *

Evo and I hike up to Lookout Point at noon. We're walking across the lawn to the lodge when I spot Jacob tossing something at a tree.

"Go ahead," I tell her, "I'll hang with Jacob."

"Male bonding?" she asks.

"I guess. He's the only kid to ever called me 'uncle.'"

"Have fun." She takes the walkway to the garden.

I head over. Jacob's throwing a tomahawk. He sticks it every other try. He tosses it the way I told him to throw the knife, like he's chopping wood. He's got a serious look, as if sticking that blade is a life-or-death matter. I like that. He's got an obsessive streak the way Jimmy did, the type of obsession that'll make him fight for the things he wants in life.

"Hey, Uncle Tony," he goes, pulling out the tomahawk.

"Choice weapon," I say.

He returns to his throwing spot. "Uncle Percy said I could borrow it. It's made for throwing."

"I see. You've graduated from knives. Very good."

We take turns. The tomahawk has a black blade with a wicked curve and a black laced grip. This is a weapon meant to do damage. Jacob tells me it came all the way from Boston and that Percy carried it across the Continental Divide.

Sarah joins us. She's wearing her mother's old peasant dress, after Kerstie shortened the hem and narrowed the waist. "Jacob," she goes, "wanna go adventuring?"

He throws the tomahawk and sticks it. "No."

"How come?"

"Still got 48 throws."

"When you've finished playing," she tells him, "you'll find me in the pantry."

*   *   *

Steve and I paddle for Cleetwood Cove in the outrigger. He's up front and I let him do most of the work. He's bare-chested and the muscles in his back flex with each pull. The sun breaks through the mist the same way it burns through the marine layer in San Diego. The caldera's rim makes me feel as if I'm in a wine glass.

Exploring the lake's fun, but you can't ignore the creep factor. You never know what you'll find, and I harbor the fear of stumbling upon a rival tribe. I wonder if Steve would have my back in a fight. He boxed in the Olympics. But boxing's one thing and survival's another. No rules in the wild. I stare into the lake. Waves off my paddle blur my reflection. A pine cone drifts by. The sky on the lake is a crisscross of wispy clouds, like lines on a chessboard.

"Sheriff Tony," Steve calls from the bow, "I'm doing all the work."

"You need the exercise, brother."

We reach the cove entrance. The drop from shore to deep blue is gradual, with shoals extending out a good 50 yards. A catamaran named *Kahuna Woman* is marooned at the tip of the cove. Aluminum posts stick out of the water, the remnants of a floating dock. Poly float sections lie on the beach. Steve tethers to a post. We wade in with rods and tackle boxes. A doe watches from shore.

"You like venison?" I ask.

"Love it," Steve answers, "but our women say hunting's verboten."

"What if our food runs out?"

"Let's keep stocking Emerald Pool," he says.

We reach the shore. Sterno cans, MRE boxes, and slats from the old dock litter the pebbles. Catgut's tangled around a life vest. A cell sits on a patch of sand. We hike a hill and pass stones stacked on a boulder. A wooden cross is wedged in the stack. We drop our gear beside the stones.

"Think anyone's here?" Steve asks.

"Not likely," I tell him.

"Why didn't they go to the lodge?"

"Maybe a rival tribe was there."

He nods. "You wanna fish or go pirating?"

I spot the restrooms on a ledge above us. "I'll pirate," I tell him, "you fish."

He unhooks Loony Spoon from an eye on his rod. "Yodel if you need me."

I watch Steve head down and return to shore before I continue. I reach a gorge that's a patchwork of whitebark pine and ponderosa. The trunks are gnarled and many are missing branches. Water cascades down a cliff. I pass a HIKERS BELOW sign, climb a wooden stairway, and reach the restrooms. The doors have been torn off and the toilet are missing. The solar panels are gone.

I head back and grab my gear. I find Steve casting where the dock used to be. Loony skips through two posts. Maybe fish hunt the water once shadowed by the dock. I cast Goldie 2. I'm not worried about dinner because Judith invited us all over for crab cakes. I reel in and cast again. Steve's pole flexes. After a short struggle, he pulls in a lump of moss. "Lord," I hear him say. Wind howls from the north off the Cascade Mountains. The pines rasp with a brittle sound, as if made of ice. It is a time of departures, a sifting away of all that can't hold on. The change is coming. I try to resist by pretending the days aren't getting shorter, that the sun isn't growing weaker. I imagine a warmer lake, the sun hot on my back. But I know the baby will come not long after the first snow. I'm worried about food and medicine. Judith will help with the birth, but what about complications? You forget about emergency rooms until you need them. Percy found five vials of liquid Amikacin in the cellar, and that's our only defense against pneumonia or other serious infections.

"Anything?" Steve calls.

"No fish in the lake," I reply.

"Head back?"

I smile. "If you do the paddling."

*   *   *

Steve drops me at Wizard Island and outriggers away through

Skell Channel. The canoe bobs in Blue Alley. I find Evo sprawled in the hammock at Lower Yurt studying a cookbook. Cosmo rests below her.

"Hey, stranger," I go.

She looks up. "Gravlaks?"

"Say what?"

"Do you like them?"

"Is that fish?"

"Salmon. Smoked and flavored with dill."

"Molto bene. Wanna go topside?"

She swings her legs off the hammock.

We hike up with Cosmo. We reach Upper Yurt and gaze out. Wind brushes the lake's surface, streaking it silver. It feels as if the past has been wiped clean and that the present is what matters. I stand behind Evo and she leans back. I wrap my arms around her. Our fingers intertwine. Her hands are small but strong.

"You and me, Tone," she whispers, "forever."

*   *   *

We're munching s'mores in front of a fire in the Great Room. I'm on the couch with Evo and Judith. The cats Zoë and Chico share a velour chair. The Snyders are camped on the bear rug in front of the crackling pine. Sarah sits on the edge of the rug beside Jacob—he examines her palm and whispers. "Am not!" Sarah giggles. Judith's crab cakes were delicious, thanks to Sarah using curry powder and oregano for seasoning. Judith shaped the patties into crescent moons before Percy deep-fried them. Now Sir Percival's on his ham radio in the pantry. I hear him shouting at fellow hammers.

Kerstie waves her tarot deck. "Any victims?" she asks.

Nobody answers. I want a reading, but I'm scared Kerstie might see something bad. Mom used to say predictions take root and sometimes come true through the power of suggestion.

"Cards are the devil's tools," Judith says.

"Are you for real?" Steve asks.

Judith gets up. "Time to retire," she goes. "Are you coming, Sarah?"

"No, Mother."

"Then, goodnight." Judith marches across the Great Room and trudges up the stairs.

Kerstie rolls her eyes.

Evo wants to be the first victim. We join the Snyders and Sarah on the rug. Evo shuffles the deck and Kerstie has her make three piles. Kerstie reforms the deck with the third pile on top and slaps cards on the maple floor. The Ace of Cups has a cup spurting water as dolphins leap. She tells Evo she will have a Capricorn girl and that the birthing will be safe. She says our child will never leave the northwest and will become a great warrior.

"I don't want that," says Evo.

"We're all warriors," goes Steve, "in one way or another."

Jacob tugs one of Sarah's lobes and she yelps.

"A warrior's cry," Jacob laughs.

Kerstie says our girl will help Oregon gain independence from a brutal enemy. Percy wanders in. He tells us there are weapon caches in Battle Ground and, if our girl wants them, he could help find them.

"Hey, Perc," I go, "slow down. She hasn't been born yet."

"Be prepared," he quips, "that's my motto."

"Boy Scouts?" I ask.

"Survivalist," he goes, "twenty-first century." He picks up our dessert plates, stacks them on his forearm, and returns to the kitchen.

I wonder what apocalypse children will be like. They must form tribes to survive and their villages should be a combo of hunters and farmers.

Kerstie says Evo will have a long life, although many of her years will be marked by struggle. The multiple Sword cards in her spread indicate conflict. Kerstie points to the Hanged Man, a man hanging by one ankle from a rope strung through a hole in a stone archway. She looks at me. I tell Kerstie he's too young to be me, but she says age is relative in tarot. She tells me to notice the man is suspended above a lake, with an island in the background.

"Christ," I mutter. "How do I get free?"

"Okay," goes Evo, "enough gloom and doom."

"Reading them how I see them," Kerstie replies. She tells Evo she's the Princess of Swords and will defend her family against all odds. She says my woman will die not long after a stranger appears, the King of Pentacles. In the card he's a dark man riding a black horse, one who holds a crystal ball with a star in it. This King is someone who travels a great distance to reach her. But this is still decades away, when Evo's hair has turned to ash.

"Next victim," goes Kerstie.

I scoot over and grab the deck. I shuffle, cut, and Kerstie stacks the cards. She slaps down ten cards, saying a connection exists between an accurate reading and a wooden surface. Jacob and Sarah get bored and take off for the kitchen. I hear them bugging Percy as he says, "Soldiers leaving Vancouver," into his microphone.

The Hanged Man reappears. Kerstie tells me danger from the lake will bind my ankle and hang me.

"Not by the neck, right?" I ask.

"No. But you'll be in a vulnerable position."

Kerstie focuses on the Chariot card in the middle of the spread and warns of forthcoming conflict and danger. Justice crosses it, and that means I must face the danger alone.

"Bummer," says Steve.

The other cards, especially the Sun, suggest a short but happy life.

"Will I see my child?" I ask.

"Give me your palm."

I hold out my right.

"Lefty?" Kerstie asks.

"Yeah."

I give her my left. She drags a fingernail from mid-palm down to my wrist. Kerstie sees another child. A son. Kerstie's blue eyes go darker, the color the lake gets near twilight.

I spot the Tower card in my spread. I figure that's not a good card with the burning tower and a man falling from a flaming window into a black abyss. "What's this Tower mean?" I ask.

"Evo will survive you," Kerstie goes.

"Enough," Evo says.

Kerstie nods and picks up the cards.

It's too late to head back to Wizard Island so Evo and I decide to spend the night. We take a room overlooking the forest. A solar light glows on the nightstand and Evo flops on the bed. "Where's Cosmo?" she asks.

"In the kitchen with Percy and the kids. They're listening to some Bostonian ramble on about a New Revolution, one with a patriot army heading south from Maine."

"Cosmo could be their mascot," Evo says.

I stare through the window. Stars sparkle above the forest and I hear a deer cry. I wonder if the approaching battle is not an outside threat but something inside me, maybe cancer or a bum heart. A ghost moon, a full moon veiled in vaporous clouds, hovers above the trees. Mom called it a Measure Moon, one that makes you think about how far you've come in life and how much further you need to go. Measure Moons make me melancholy. I want my years to count. When I was young I threw time away because it seemed endless. Dadio warned me we're only here from spring to fall.

"Penny for your thoughts," Evo calls from bed.

"Please promise," I tell her, "promise you'll never forget me."

"Not for a minute of my life."

OUTSIDERS

OCTOBER 23rd ARRIVES. The day's humid but the sky's clear. Goldie 2 is in need of repair after a bully brown twisted her dorsal hook. I cast a feather into Blue Alley. Ducks land in Emerald Pool. Cosmo snaps at bees on the shore. Salamanders bask on stones and pink blossoms shimmer under the pines. The crater's still warm enough to wear trunks. The creel hangs off my shoulder, and I've got the binos tucked inside. The hemlock and whitebark are netted in shadow, and the birds that once nested in their branches have left. I swat at a bug that hums like a mosquito. I feel a pull stronger than the usual current but it's not a bite. I look out to where my line punctures the water and see a strand of moss trailing after the feather. I reel in, pull off the moss, and cast again. The lake feels like a friend today. Other times it seems foreign. My cards warned danger would come from the water, and I imagine Nessie surfacing to swallow me whole.

Cosmo barks.

I reel in. "Hey, champ," I call, "who you barking at?"

His ears twitch. I smell exhaust. I put my rod down and pull out the binos. I spot the green hull of Steve's outrigger as he paddles for

Phantom Ship with Kerstie. Jacob's not with them. Bet he's up at the lodge with Sarah. They're in that holding hands phase. I suspect torrid make-out sessions during their unsupervised hikes. Jacob just turned fourteen. Sarah will be thirteen on Christmas day. They've circled the crater rim and trekked the entire shore of the lake. They know every inlet, bay, and alcove. They showed me a secret path from the crater shore up to Lookout Point that takes half-an-hour. Jacob wants Sarah to bike with him to K Falls but Kerstie won't allow it.

"Percy to Tony," my walkie-talkie crackles. "You there, Sheriff?"

I zip open my fanny pack. "What's up, Perc?"

"Haywire Elzie in K Falls sends an SOS. He swears, as God is his Maker, that an F-450 blew through town searching for a white Rover. Guy at the wheel asked if Highway 97 was best for Crater Lake."

"How long ago?"

"Four hours, maybe five."

"How many?"

"Three or four nasties. Driver was packing. Towing a boat."

I flash back to the dome, with Evo at the blinds. Bikers circle the hen house. Dave comes out. Cosmo's barking hard. I tap the Panther's trigger.

"Tony," goes Percy's voice. "You still there?"

I swallow hard. "Yeah."

"Watch Danger Bay. That's the only place to launch."

"Is Evo at the lodge?"

"Sure is. Picking tomatoes."

"Don't let her out of your sight. Load the 12-gauge. Where are the others?"

"Judith's with me in the pantry. Sarah and Jacob are at Lookout Point."

"Get the kids back to the lodge. Lock all windows and doors. Tell Evo to get Super Shorty. Don't panic if you hear gunshots."

"You got it, Sheriff."

I take a deep breath. I slip the walkie-talkie back in my fanny pack. My heart races. I barefoot it to Lower Yurt and lift the Panther out from the lava crevice. I pull on my hiking boots, lace them tight, and charge for Upper Yurt with Cosmo. A hemlock branch scrapes my neck. I reach Upper Yurt and stare out over a lake so calm it seems like a painting. No boat. No men. No stink of exhaust. Ducks squawk below in Emerald Pool.

I climb higher. Bone-white trunks at the top of the cone surround me. I jog to the eastern edge and see snow geese flocking in Cleetwood Cove. An engine whines. I raise the binos, sweep east, and zero in on a gray Zodiac thrashing a whitewater trail out of Danger Bay. A man with a red do-rag is crouched at the bow. Two share the stern—one's beanpole-thin and the other's got his hand on the shifter. The Zodiac angles northwest, cutting straight for Wizard Island. I lower the binos. I crank the Panther's bolt and load the chamber. I scope the Zodiac. I should sink it and pick the men off in the lake. But I can't fire.

The Zodiac makes Fumarole Bay. I check out Phantom Ship and see Kerstie hiking. I return to the Zodiac: it's cruising the shoals. The man at the bow barks orders. That must be Joe. "Land, you bastards," I mutter, knowing I'll have them contained on the island. "Let trouble come to you," Dadio told me, "don't go looking for it." Cosmo nudges me with his nose and I pat him. "Ready for some action, boy?"

The walkie-talkie crackles. "Evo wants to canoe over, Sheriff."

I pull it out. "Tell her to stay put, Perc."

"You know Evo. Headstrong and all."

"Listen, Percy. She can't help. I've got this wired."

"Tony?" goes Evo.

"Je-sus," I mumble. I bury the walkie-talkie under the cinders. I scope down and find Joe on the bow. He points. The driver steers the Zodiac into an inlet near Emerald Pool. Their keel bumps a submerged stepping stone, and Joe nearly falls in the lake. The Zodiac maroons. Joe makes a slashing motion and the driver kills the engine. Joe pushes them free with an oar and they drift toward shore. Beanpole hops out and tethers the Zodiac. The driver follows Joe out and hands Beanpole a shotgun. Joe's toting a carbine with a banana clip. The driver passes more weapons, including pistols and a riot gun. Joe's wearing a leather vest and his belly hangs over his jeans like a sack of barley. He sticks chaw in his mouth and picks up a discarded MRE box. Beanpole hurls a stone at Emerald Pool—the ducks take flight. The driver throws my rod into the lake.

The driver leads the way up to Lower Yurt holding the riot gun. He's got a Fu Man Chu and wears a Rangers baseball cap. Joe's right behind, and Beanpole brings up the rear. All three wear boots.

I go prone, resting the Panther on a dead branch jutting out of the cinders. Cosmo hunkers down beside me. I scope. Joe's got an automatic pistol wedged in his vest and has a knife tucked in a belted sheath. Beanpole's holding a shotgun.

The driver stumbles and the riot gun clangs on the ground. "Shit," he says.

"Clumsy ass," Joe grouches.

They hit mid-trail and sneak up to Lower Yurt. The driver charges in brandishing the riot gun. Joe pulls his pistol and waits outside. The driver leaves the yurt and wanders over to the Coleman stove. He touches the burners. Joe disappears into the yurt but soon emerges with a photo album. Beanpole flops in the hammock. Joe yanks Beanpole out by the hair, flings him off, and takes his place. Joe leafs through the album as Beanpole rocks him.

Who should I kill first? Joe's a slob and zero challenge. Beanpole's a wimp. I crosshair the driver's chest. "Goodnight, Irene."

Cosmo runs into my line of fire and charges down the cone

252

barking.

"Back, boy," I plead, "come, Cosmo."

He returns and I pull him down. I scope again—no sign of the men. The hammock rocks. Someone's scrambling toward Upper Yurt. It's Beanpole. He reaches the yurt, raises his shotgun, and charges in.

I scope back to Lower Yurt. The driver knocks over the Coleman stove and pisses on the yurt's wall. "Anybody home?" he shouts up to Beanpole.

"Nope!"

The driver prods the solar shower's black bag with his riot gun.

I'm sweating like a demon. My hands shake and my shooting eye waters. I crosshair the Ranger cap and pull. The Panther *ba-rooms* and the butt slams my shoulder. The black bag bursts and showers the driver. My second shot drops him. Return fire forces me down and Cosmo takes off. I crawl south and scope. No sign of Beanpole or Joe.

I hear footsteps behind me.

"Move and you die," comes a squeaky voice.

A barrel's tip smacks me between the shoulders like a fist.

"Hands off that elephant gun and get up, nice and easy like."

I leave the Panther on the cinders and stand. He's still behind me with the barrel jammed against my spine.

"Hands behind your back and wrists together."

I do as I'm told. I get cuffed.

"Face me."

I turn around. Beanpole's holding his shotgun low and close. His dirty blond hair looks greasy, and he smells like rotten hamburger. Cosmo watches from beside the camouflage tent. I look past a cluster of ghost trunks and see the canoe knifing through Fumarole Bay.

Joe breaches the edge of the cone with his carbine. The automatic pistol bulges out his vest. "Dude," he goes, "where you been all my life?"

"You Joe?"

He chews tobacco the way a cow chews cud. "Sure am," he says. "Bet that grill on your Rover's stuffed with desert bugs."

I say nothing.

Joe spits tobacco juice. "You got lucky, dude, headin' north. But your lucky streak's over." He signals with his eyes and Beanpole scoots behind me.

Joe pulls his pistol. The cinders crunch under his boots as he approaches. "Somethin' I've been a-hankerin' to ask you, dude. Fact is, I drove a thousand to ask it. Found my baby bro in Pinyon Crest, body a-crawlin' maggots and head rolled down in the gulch. Took all afternoon piecin' Royce back. No way to go, let alone kin. You do it?"

"Royce and his pals murdered my friend."

"Dude," he snaps, "am I askin' who or when or what or how or why? No. What I'm askin' is this—you kill 'im?"

"He got what was coming."

Joe pistol-whips my face.

I fall to my knees. I'm sure he broke my cheekbone.

"Nephew," Joe says, "let's have a lil' fun."

Cosmo whines beside the tent. Joe fires his carbine and Cosmo races out of the dimple. "Hate fleabags," Joe says.

"Motherfucker," I go, tugging against the cuffs. The harder I tug, the deeper the steel bites into my wrists.

"You kill Royce?" Joe presses.

"Fuck yes."

"Get 'im on his feet, nephew."

Beanpole grabs the cuffs and yanks me up.

"Cousin Ajax filled us in," Joe tells me, "shoots the shit about this babe prancin' at his bar and how he gassed a white Rover. Seems that same Rover passed me in Pinyon Crest. Followed the breadcrumbs to Pismo, up to San Fran, and over to K Falls. Now you're cuffed on an island in the middle of a lake."

"You're a bloodhound, uncle," pipes up Beanpole.

"What happened to Nirvana?" I ask.

Joe spits. "Torched that hippie nest, after blastin' them darn chickens and slittin' open those goats."

"You sonuvabitch."

"Where's your hot lady at?"

"Vancouver."

"You're fibbin'."

Beanpole slams the shotgun's butt into my kidney. I double over.

Joe smirks. "Bet she's at that lodge sippin' mint juleps."

"I want her," Beanpole says.

"All in good time, nephew," goes Joe. He slides a knuckle buster knife out of his sheath. "Let's do to him what we done to that Injun." He sticks his sausage fingers through the slots of the knife's brass knuckle handle. Each slot in the handle has a barb.

"First dibs," Beanpole begs. "You owe me, uncle."

"Owe you for what?"

"Was me found that Injun under the roulette table."

"Fair's fair," Joe says, extending the knuckle buster. "You first."

Beanpole hustles over and grabs it.

"Save some for your uncle."

Beanpole threads his fingers through the brass knuckles. He grins and saunters over to me. His teeth are the color of piss. He whacks my face—the barbs shoot into my cheek like nails. I topple backwards and fall.

"That felt good," Beanpole crows, "was it a good one, uncle?"

"Damn fine, nephew. You make me proud."

I try getting to my feet but can't. I spit blood. Beanpole tugs me up by the hair and smashes the knuckles into my nose.

"Cut 'im," Joe says.

Beanpole slips the blade under my tank top. He jerks the knife and the fabric splits. He slashes my chest. Blood spurts down to my belly. He slices open my forearm. I enter a fog from the torture. I flash to Peanut, my boyhood turtle, floating dead in her tank. I smell blood on the cinders and gaze over the cone. The crater looks like a cathedral rising into the sky and I remember it raining during Jimmy's burial, and huddling with Dadio under an umbrella. Something moves through the ghost trees. Blows rain on my temple and I fall face down.

"Can I take an eye, uncle?"

"Did we take the Injun's?"

"Frank took both, then squashed 'em under his boot."

"Do it, nephew."

I squirm away and bury my face in the cinders. The knife enters my upper lid as Beanpole tries carving through the flesh below the eyebrow.

"The hard way," Joe coaches.

"How, uncle?"

"Jam that blade into his temple and peel back like your skinnin' an orange."

A *ba-room* rattles my eardrums. I turn over and look up—the knuckle buster heads skyward with fingers still threaded through the brass knuckles. The knife and severed hand return, splattering on a stump. Beanpole cries like a girl.

Someone with a blurred face stands over me. The smell of burnt gunpowder helps me focus on a savage brown face with feminine features. It's Evo. "Don't look so hot, Tone," she goes.

I roll to one side and prop myself up with an elbow. I see Joe raising his rifle.

"Look out!" I warn.

A *packa-pop* blows off Joe's do-rag. A second *packa-pop* makes him drop his carbine and tumble over.

Beanpole uses his stump like a crutch to stand. He reaches for his holstered gun.

A tomahawk sails through the sky as if thrown by a god. It *thwanks* into Beanpole, lodging in his upper back. He tugs at the handle but the blade's in too deep. He stumbles off with Cosmo snapping at his legs. "Get off!" he cries as fangs sink in. Beanpole falls off the cone's eastern side, where a wicked lava ravine and hemlocks wait. I hear him somersaulting down through the trees.

Jacob flashes me a thumbs up and tucks the Beretta back in his shoulder holster. He nabs the carbine and aims it at Joe. Joe throws him the automatic pistol.

Evo pulls her Swiss Army knife and selects a blade. She picks at the lock in my cuffs.

"So, this is our babe," Joe calls over. "I'm Joe and you're?"

"Evo," she tells him. "Gimme the key."

"What's my reward, Evo?"

"Five extra minutes to live."

Joe gets up. He pulls a key from his vest and tosses it to her.

She catches the key and sticks it in the lock.

I hear a click and the cuffs swing open. I get to my knees and stand. I'm free.

"Evo," Joe calls.

"What?"

"Me and your dude need to settle up mano-a-mano."

Evo sashays over with Super Shorty and sticks the barrel in his face.

"Don't let her fuck me up, dude! Lemme go out a man."

Lordy, I think. I'm certain this is that Royce dare, the Gladiators in the Coliseum bull. No dice. I'm not falling for that again. Joe's at my mercy. My cheek and nose throb. Blood streams from my face. I'll need a hundred stitches. Sweat makes the wounds sting.

"You know what I'm sayin', dude," Joe begs. "You and Royce went mano-a-mano and you made his head roll. Don't I deserve that same respect?"

I know I can take this bastard. He looks weak balancing his weight on one leg. His paunch hangs over his belt and he seems like a harmless old uncle. Why shouldn't I honor his last request? I flash to Kerstie's cards, remembering her warning that I must face danger alone. If I don't, Evo and our baby could get cursed. I imagine that I'm on the crater rim raising a red blade to honor the spirit of the lake.

"Evo," I say, "bring the Tuareg from Lower Yurt. Look under the quilt."

"Don't do it, Uncle Tony," Jacob pleads.

"Tony," goes Evo, "this guy could kill you."

"I want the family cutlass," Joe barks, "on my boat."

"Get the dagger and the cutlass," I tell Evo.

"Forget it."

Jacob waves the carbine. "I'll go, Uncle Tony."

"Fly like the wind, boy."

Jacob zips by with Cosmo in hot pursuit. He dodges pines, slips between boulders, and kicks up dust sprinting the cinder path.

Evo prowls near Joe aiming Super Shorty. I wonder how many women have witnessed their husbands in a fight to the death. The monster inside me stirs. I'm suddenly craving combat and blood.

"You desert folk?" Joe asks.

"Vista," I answer. "San Diego County. You?"

"Atlanta."

Evo gives him the evil eye.

Jacob returns with the weapons. I remove the Tuareg's nickel sheath and swing the dagger-like blade. It's not too light and not too heavy. The handle doesn't feel slippery even though drops of my blood and sweat hit the leather.

"Here's the cutlass," Jacob tells me. He holds out a short stubby scabbard with a cloth inlay.

"Give it to Joe."

Jacob brings him the cutlass.

Joe yanks on the pommel and rips off the scabbard. His blade is thick and slightly longer than the Tuareg. He tosses the scabbard and slashes the air. "What kinda blade you got?" he asks me.

"A Tuareg," I tell him, "from North Africa."

Joe chuckles. "Africans can't make blades."

"You'll soon discover how good they are."

"Hey, Joe," goes Evo, "when Tony takes your head, will Ajax come?"

"Sure will, unless I return to Satan's Barb."

"You and Ajax," I say, "are both cowards."

A devil-like scowl sweeps over Joe's face. His eyes burn. "Yah!" he goes, charging. He flails with the cutlass, and the Tuareg blocks a downward swipe. He takes the fight to me with an onslaught of thrusts and slashes. Evo shadows the action like a ref. Joe swings the cutlass, and the fat blade nicks my forearm.

Evo raises Super Shorty. "Game over," she goes, "drop the cutlass, Joe."

"Last day on Earth!" he spouts.

"Bring it on," I tell him.

Joe lashes out with the stubby blade. The rage has left his face, and his blows are getting weaker. He's favoring a leg and breathing hard. I go gladiator, raining down blow upon blow. He blocks them all, except for a swipe to shoulder that feels like I've hacked into meat with a cleaver. He stumbles back. Blood shoots down his arm and splatters the ground. He holds his blade low. I see the hole in his jeans where Jacob's bullet struck. He raises the cutlass and I dodge a vicious swing. I get in an upward slash that splits open his vest. He retreats. "Stuck me good," he admits, taking a deep breath. He charges unexpectedly and we're blade to blade, the lean Tuareg grinding into the thick steel of the cutlass. I spread my legs for leverage and inch my blade toward his jugular. He slides a boot between my legs, slams my chest with a fist, and I fall backwards.

Joe raises the cutlass with both hands on the pommel. "This is for Royce!"

A *ba-room* lifts Joe off his feet. He lands in a heap with his eyes open and hands clutching the pommel. He stares into the sky as dust swirls around his body.

*   *   *

Steve and Kerstie outrigger over to Wizard Island. Jacob canoes Skell Channel to get Percy and Judith. The walkie-talkies are invaluable. Evo tells Judith to bring everything and anything to patch me. Thank god for Dave's clotting sponge, the sutures, the antiseptic, and the bandages. I slug Jack Daniels while Judith stitches me in Upper Yurt. I feel like Raggedy Andy as I lie on a layer of yoga mats. Sarah dabs my face with antiseptic and Judith starts stitching the wounds in my cheek. She says my cheekbone's chipped and that my nose is busted. The nick from the cutlass is only superficial but still needs stitches. Judith soldiers on with her stitching. Steve can't watch. He grabs the binos and leaves to scout the lake.

Judith works through the night. Solar and propane lamps keep Upper Yurt bright. Blood trickles out from between the sutures in my chest. The forearm wound is deeper than I thought. I'm at 124 stitches when Judith knots my last one. "Good as new, Tony," says Judith.

I turn to Evo. "Am I scary, Babe?"

She nods. "You're a dead ringer for Frankenstein."

*   *   *

I rock on a hickory chair outside the lodge. Percy and Steve rock too. It's mid-afternoon and we're swilling Guinness. Steve lights a clove cigarette from that duffel bag I snagged from Ryan way back in Portico. Percy tells us a leader has emerged from Tangiers, a woman pirate who stole a tanker and smashed through a blockade in the Strait of Gibraltar to free thousands of prisoners. Countless battles rage in the new world, including one in San Diego pitting an army of Scientologists against renegade patriots led by a man who lost his daughter to a zealot. I wonder if Abraham is involved.

Joe was our first test. We passed, but barely. Snow will fall soon and block the roads to Crater Lake. The last of the fawn lilies have blossomed and withered. New birds, those able to withstand harsh winters, have replaced the familiar ones.

A week has passed since Joe's visit. But I'm not finished with him. His stiff carcass lies on top of Wizard Island. Beanpole's somewhere in the ravine. Steve already dragged the driver's body down to the shore.

"What's the plan, Stan?" Steve asks, blowing smoke.

"A pyre?" I suggest.

"Their ashes could pollute the lake."

Percy quits rocking. "Eureka," he says, "I've got it!" He gulps his last swallow of Guinness, pops off his rocker, and runs for the lodge.

Steve stomps out his butt. "Want your Beretta back?"

"Give it to your sharp-shooting son. Remember our stash: a riot gun that fires slugs, three shotguns, a carbine, and a pair of automatic pistols. Take the carbine."

"I can't even load a gun."

"Jacob can. Besides, it's never too late to teach an old dog new tricks."

"You and Percy are the oldest, Tony."

I feel like a coward hanging out at the lodge. The outsiders want me. Ajax will come and, when he does, he could hurt the others. It would be safer for them if Evo and I split. But where would we go? Heading south would be suicide. North would be brutal with winter at our doorstep. Should I go alone and leave Evo behind?

Percy returns with boxes of tire chains. "Let's chain those bastards together," he tells us, "and sink them in the lake."

Steve shakes his head. "Not a chance," he goes. "They'd rot and poison the water."

"The sun won't reach them," I tell Steve. "It's like putting them on ice for eternity."

*   *   *

We take the Zodiac to Wizard Island. We have plenty of fuel in the can to feed the outboard. Percy finds Beanpole's body and we drag him and Joe down to shore. We chain them to the driver. I'm surprised how easy it is to secure the chains with metal hooks meant for tires.

Jacob canoes over. Steve tells him not to land. We roll the chained bodies into the Zodiac and it nearly flips accepting their weight. We move the bodies to the middle and place them horizontal to help balance the Zodiac. Steve and I stuff their pockets with stones.

"I'll go back with Jacob," Percy says. He frees our mooring line and shoves the Zodiac out.

Steve and I drift from shore.

Blood trickles down my chest, staining my old Izod. I must have tweaked the sutures. I yank the starter cord—the engine doesn't turn over. I squeeze a little black ball that feeds fuel into the outboard through a red hose. I yank again. The bonnet rattles. I squeeze the ball again and a third yank has the engine purring. I steer through Fumarole Bay. Steve stands on a wooden platform at the bow to keep the Zodiac from bouncing. I cut the small waves at an angle. I worry we're floating too low. The chains on the bodies are streaked with rust. I can't look at their faces. The sun hangs near the western rim and light threads through the pines. I gaze behind the boat and see the propeller churning a trail of turquoise bubbles.

"This is the middle," Steve says.

"Farther," I tell him, increasing our speed a few notches. The bow lifts. A log drifts through the purple water. Ahead, snow geese line the shore of Cleetwood Cove.

Steve peers down. "How deep is it?"

"A thousand feet," I go, shifting to idle. "Let's sink these devils."

We turn the bodies perpendicular. Steve helps me lift Joe up and over the gunwale. His body floats. His weight counterbalances the others and helps us hoist out the driver and Beanpole. There's a monstrous splash. The Zodiac rocks so violently that we need to crouch to avoid falling. The boat stabilizes. I get up and look down: the chained men drift through purple into the dark abyss, forever entwined.

EPILOGUE

A CANADIAN STORM swept in on November 9th, the week Percy stowed our solar generators. The shores were blanketed with a bluish snow that reminded me of Arctic glaciers. The wind was fierce and constant for days, knocking icicles off the lodge's eaves and rousting birds from the hemlocks. Tundra swans took flight. I'd wanted to tough it out on Wizard Island but realized the yurt could smother us in snow if the roof collapsed. Besides, it was bone cold behind those canvas walls, even with two propane heaters blazing. Steve helped me tear down Upper and Lower Yurt. We built a hemlock shanty beside Emerald Pool to store the yurts and camping gear.

The lodge's meadows became the Land of Shadows. Wildflowers melted away. A few crowns of broccoli and clumps of winter squash were all that remained of our garden. Another storm hit on Turkey Day and six-foot drifts kept us sealed inside. We played Twister and Monopoly in the Great Room. The fireplace raged with burning logs and Evo made Irish coffees. Percy surprised us by breaking out his violin and playing Beethoven's *Fidelio*, something he'd learned from his maestro father in Boston. Judith baked a turkey Percy had stowed in the cellar.

*   *   *

Evo likes knee-length dresses. I've never found pregnant women attractive but she changed my mind. Sometimes she models her blue bandage dress from the Ghost Bar. She craves smoked herring. Our room's on the top floor and it has a sweeping view from the lake to the forest. We have a stone fireplace, lithium lamps, and Navajo rugs.

We still fish, but never with rod and reel. A gill net is anchored off Fumarole Bay that Jacob checks between storms. Between that net and the trout he scoops out of Emerald Pool we have plenty of fish. I tease Jacob into snowball fights and we play football with Steve. When we come in from the cold, Kerstie serves us hot chocolate and strudel.

*   *   *

Cosmo likes chasing Zoë and Chico through the lobby. It drives Percy loco. Sometimes Jacob and Sarah ride their bikes in the Great Room. We've got plenty of canned goods and MREs. Steve built a lean-to beside the garden. That's where we store salted salmon and trout. We still have hot water, thanks to Percy's plumbing expertise and Steve's gas generator. I siphoned thirty gallons from Joe's truck to keep the generator humming. I found a Polaroid of me and Evo on his dash, the one Dave took of us inside the dome.

My daily regimen keeps me active. I split logs for firewood each morning, wood from dead timber. I shovel snow off the walkways all the way to Lookout Point. I scout for outsiders.

The women cook. Evo and Kerstie have this Scandinavian-cuisine contest going. It's Norway vs. Sweden every night. Kerstie started things off by making Swedish meatballs in cream sauce with scalloped potatoes. Evo countered with rakfisk, a fermented trout over crepe pancakes. Kerstie struck back with Svenska fisksoppa, a thick fish soup with garlic, tarragon, and basil. Evo topped that with Fersk suppe, a horseradish soup loaded with onions and nutmeg-spiced cabbage. Their competition includes desserts. Evo spent all morning slaving over krumkake, a paper-thin rolled cake topped with whipped cream. Kerstie responded with Prinsesstårta, a large sponge cake layered with custard. The men vote for their favorites to fan the flames of competition. We dine in the Great Room every night, after joining hands and saying prayers of gratitude. We talk about everything from ancestors to hopes and dreams for the future. Kerstie tells Viking tales. Evo shares her teenage summers camping in Bergen, Norway. Steve boasts about his adventures on the Vltava River from Vienna to Prague, and the years captaining a ferry from Ventspils to St. Petersburg. Percy has great lake stories, such as secret islands appearing on the lake at sunset and disappearing by sunrise. Jacob and Sarah hold hands during our ramblings.

*   *   *

I worried that everyone would get bored at the lodge. I was wrong. Kerstie paints scenes of the lake. Evo writes fables. Judith and Sarah make quilts. Percy gives Jacob violin lessons. I keep a journal. Steve's hobby is bird watching and recording new arrivals. We'll have to get accustomed to being indoors for most of the next five months. I've set up a Sentry Suite on the top floor. The men take turns watching Crater Rim Road. We've got a spyglass, binos, and night vision goggles. I keep the Panther there too.

The Snyders never want to leave. I don't blame them. I have discovered the simple pleasures make life worth living: the aroma of wood crackling in the fireplace, deer calling at twilight, stars above the caldera, and sharing my days with Evo and good friends.

*   *   *

I need to figure things out before others arrive. The approaching Solstice gives me time. Crater Lake Road is already an impenetrable white blanket. But outsiders will come. Tribes from Medford or K Falls could brave the snow and challenge us. If we need to run, Rovy can breach the steep lava. Percy says only a few will reach Crater Lake and, when they do, they might make us stronger. "The Crater Lake Gang," he kids. Sometimes the lodge feels too big for us and that we should share it. I imagine happy voices drifting up from the Great Room and children playing in the meadows.

*   *   *

Judith takes Evo's pulse, examines her eyes, and sticks a fetal stethoscope against her belly. "Strong heartbeat," goes Judith. Sarah wants to help. Good thing Judith brought her mid-wife kit, one that includes antiseptic, forceps, cord clamps, sutures, irrigation bottles, and even an infant resuscitator. Percy chipped in by carving a birthing stool out of birch.

*   *   *

It's sunrise. We're a week from Winter Solstice. Evo stands at our window. I sneak up from behind and wrap my arms around her. I cup her belly with my palms. I feel a kick. We watch a doe and two fawns nibble on branches jutting out from the snow.

Evo strokes my arm. "Are we safe, Tone?"

"Yes."

I flash to a past of mortgage payments, mindless entertainment, and driving from home to work and back again. Now the twenty-first century wavers between darkness and hope.

The aroma of fresh pastry drifts up from the lobby. I feel another kick. Warblers land on the lodge's façade and peck at the lava. I see Jacob in the Land of Shadows—he's tossing Cosmo a tennis ball while Sarah looks on. Steve's on a rocker having a smoke. Percy and Judith stroll toward Lookout Point.

The trees on Wizard Island resemble vanilla Popsicles. Snow geese and tundra swans have gathered in Fumarole Bay. The cobalt bay is calm. There's an eerie quiet, the way it gets before a storm. The crater walls arch like vaults in a Gothic cathedral. I thank Dave for Crater Lake. He knew it wasn't the water that would keep us safe. It was the snow. Snow to smother roads and cover our tracks. Snow to discourage outsiders. I promise him I'll be there for Cosmo. I remember our last dinner with the view of the mesas and clouds drifting over the Mojave like renegade balloons.

"Look, Tone," Evo whispers.

The geese and swans rise off Fumarole Bay. I hear wings brushing air as the two species merge into a single flock. They become a brilliant white cloud over Wizard Island and hold their form against the blue.

ABOUT THE AUTHOR

Kirby Wright was born and raised in Honolulu, Hawaii. He is a graduate of Punahou School in Honolulu and the University of California at San Diego. He received his MFA in Creative Writing from San Francisco State University. Wright has been nominated for four Pushcart Prizes and is a past recipient of the *Honolulu Weekly* Prizes in Poetry and Nonfiction, the Jodi Stutz Memorial Prize in Poetry, the Ann Fields Poetry Prize, the Academy of American Poets Award, the Robert Browning Award for Dramatic Monologue, and Arts Council Silicon Valley Fellowships in Poetry and The Novel. BEFORE THE CITY, his first poetry collection, took First Place at the 2003 San Diego Book Awards. Wright is also the author of the companion novels PUNAHOU BLUES and MOLOKA'I NUI AHINA, both set in Hawaii. He was a Visiting Fellow at the 2009 International Writers Conference in Hong Kong, where he represented the Pacific Rim region of Hawaii. He was also a Visiting Writer at the 2010 Martha's Vineyard Residency in Edgartown, Mass., and the 2011 Artist in Residence at Milkwood International, Czech Republic.